Also by Tim Chapman

Bright and Yellow, Hard and Cold

KIDDIELAND
and other misfortunes

Stories by Tim Chapman

Author of *Bright and Yellow, Hard and Cold*

Thrilling Tales
Chicago, IL

Thrilling Tales
Chicago, IL

www.thrillingtales.com

This is a work of fiction. Descriptions and portrayals of real people, events, organizations, or establishments are intended to provide background for the story and are used fictitiously. Other characters and situations are drawn from the author's imagination and are not intended to be real.

© 2014 by Tim Chapman
All rights reserved

Book and cover design by Tim Chapman

ISBN: 978-0-9862862-0-9

Library of Congress Control Number: 2014921056

Many thanks to the editors at The Southeast Review, the Chicago Reader, Alfred Hitchcock's Mystery Magazine, Chicago Tribune's Printers Row Journal, Hectoin International, and the anthology, *The Rich and the Dead* where several of these stories previously appeared.

For Ellen

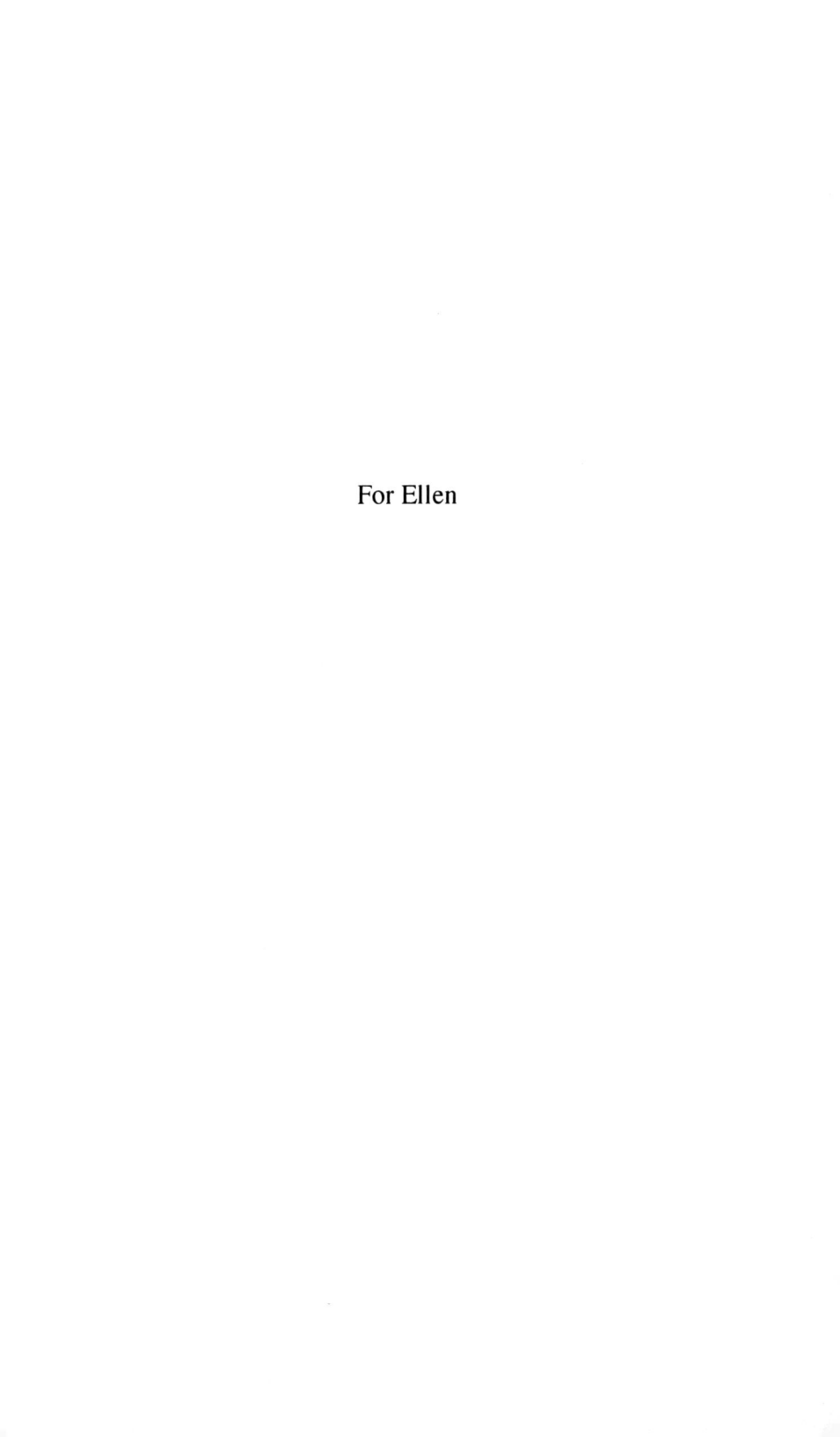

INTRODUCTION

The stories in this collection cover a diverse range of themes and genres. There are detective stories, love stories, and even a sci-fi tale. There are short stories and short-short stories ("Downsizing" was a finalist in the 2006 World's Best Short-Short Story competition). I like story collections that try to tell a larger story by connecting characters or themes from one story to the next. *Olive Kitteridge* is a good example of a book like that. This is not.

I suppose the thing that ties these stories together is that these fictional characters, like us, are wondering what it's all about. Events occur in our lives over which we seem to have no control. If we see these events as having a favorable outcome, we congratulate ourselves for our brilliance and foresight. If, on the other hand, the outcome is not to our liking, we shake our fists at the heavens and curse our luck. These, then, are stories about how we respond to unforseen events.

Art, science, religion, and philosophy are all ways in which humans ask questions about our place in the universe. Asking is what differentiates living from existing. Asking is good; worrying is not. I take comfort in the knowledge that the only thing we can know for certain is that we can't know anything for certain. To borrow a phrase from Bruce Lee—be like water my friend.

Tim Chapman
Chicago 2014

CONTENTS

ADVERSITY

DEAR HART	15
SECRET GARDEN	25
A SOFT PERSISTENT RAIN	41
A CLOSER WALK WITH THEE	45
FISH STORY	61
DOWNSIZING	71
THE WIND	73
HERO COMPLEX	83

ANXIETY

THE GENTILE GRIFT	93
DANCE LESSON	107
A FLASH OF LIGHTNING	113
STIGMATA	125
THE METAL TEETH OF THE MONSTER	135
FEAR	139
THE END OF SUMMER	143
WHAT STAYS	147

CRIMINALITY

THE SEED	151
DIRTY WATER	175
EASY PIECE	183
A BLADE OF GRASS	199
WHAT WE DO FOR LOVE	203
SEVEN	209
KIDDIELAND	213

ADVERSITY

DEAR HART

  Karin couldn't tell anyone why she wanted the divorce. She knew why, but it wasn't a reason that anyone else would understand, so she blamed it on "irreconcilable differences." It didn't matter that David and all their friends continually asked what the irreconcilable differences were, she just shook her head and repeated her mantra. She felt bad for David. It wasn't really his fault, and he was so obviously bewildered. She felt bad about not being able to tell her father, too, but there was no way in hell he would have understood. She hadn't yet told her girlfriends though she knew she'd have to sooner or later. They all liked her husband, so she expected them to be ambivalent about her decision, at best. It was times like this when she missed her mother. The woman who had died two days before Karin's eighteenth birthday would have understood how even the most sincere love could vanish, practically overnight. It had been six years, and she hadn't found anyone she could talk with the way she and her mother had talked.
  She was silent on the drive to couple's counseling.

She wasn't angry with David and certainly wasn't trying to punish him. She just felt that talking in front of an objective third party was safer. That was, she realized, one of the reasons she agreed to go to these counseling sessions. The other was to leave David with the feeling that he had tried his best. She knew him well enough to know that he'd blame himself for the ruination of their marriage. Maybe this would help to alleviate some of his guilt. She certainly hoped so.

She listened to him as he drove and wished he would stop trying to sound cheerful, as though his upbeat chatter could fix them.

"So, how about that Dr. Paretta? She's nice and all but, come on, does having a PhD really mean you get to call yourself a doctor? Not that I'm complaining. If anyone can help us through this little rough patch... I mean, she seems like she knows her stuff, doesn't she?"

Karin didn't answer. One question answered would lead to another asked, and then it would be like a pebble rolling down a hill, gaining momentum and picking up other pebbles along the way until they knocked loose the giant, fucking boulder-sized question she couldn't answer. She turned her head just enough so she could stare out the window at the snow-shrouded countryside without appearing to deliberately turn away from her husband. That was the impression she had hoped to convey, but in her peripheral vision she saw the corners of his mouth turn down.

The drive south to Madison was just a little over an hour, and in the summer it was a corridor of bold greens and rolling hills occasionally interrupted by fields of grazing cows. She loved the cows. Their gentle-looking eyes and slow saunters made her think they were the most sympathetic creatures on earth. Even dolphins came in a distant second to cows. She thought dolphins were too smart for their own good, the lousy show-offs.

In winter the terrain was different. The white of the snow blended into the gray of the sky so you couldn't tell where one left off and the other began. Leafless trees stretched out their skeletal branches. After the occasional ice storm they looked like they had been dipped in glaze. In the weeks leading up to Christmas, Karin agreed with the rest of the Midwest that this was charming—a "winter wonderland." By the second week in January the landscape seemed harsh and forbidding, and by February it just seemed dangerous. The livestock that were foolish enough to wander out to the fields looked cold and uncomfortable to her, the cows shuffling stiff-legged through the snow drifts.

Dr. Paretta really wasn't much help. Her main contribution was rephrasing what Karin's husband had just said and asking her how she felt about it. What David had to say was accurate enough. He was considerate and supportive. He helped out around the house and would occasionally bring her little gifts. Just last weekend he had stopped at the grocery on his way home from a hunting trip and picked up a pint of the Chunky Monkey ice cream she was so fond of. She had no complaints about their sex life. Karin agreed that he was a fine husband. She just couldn't explain to him, or to Dr. Paretta, why she no longer wanted to be his wife. Or live with him. Or, for that matter, be in the same room with him.

"I'm sorry," she said, addressing both of them.

"Sorry for what?" Dr. Paretta asked.

Karin stared at the gray carpet between her feet. "Just sorry."

o

Thankfully, the bar was empty, so Karin and her friends didn't have to raise their voices to be heard. They had marched straight to the back booth, and Vicky had gone up to the bar to put in their order while Denise hung up the coats. Both women were being solicitous, having decided that Karin's husband must have been abusive. They wanted her to know that they were there for her, and told her so.

"We're here for you," Denise said. "You can count on us."

Vicky came back from the bar with a pitcher of appletinis and three glasses. She slid into the booth next to Denise, giving her a little hip bump. "Scoot over, babe."

Denise slid across the booth, turning to lean against the knotty pine paneling.

"What are we talking about?" Vicky asked.

"I was just saying that we'll support Karin in whatever she decides. That's what friends do, support each other."

"Of course we will," Vicky agreed. She took a sip of her drink and reached across the table to give Karin's hand a little squeeze. "Has it been awful? I would never have guessed that you two were having problems. You always seemed like the perfect couple to me."

"Me too," Denise said. "Not like me and my ex. Now there was a train wreck waiting to happen." She looked at Karin's untouched appletini. "Does he drink? Mine did."

Karin shook her head. "No. It's really my problem. He hasn't done anything."

Vicky snorted. "That sounds like somebody in denial. Did he hit you? No, don't tell me." She held up her hand. "Even if he didn't hit you there are plenty of other types of abuse. You don't owe anybody an explanation."

Denise asked, "Does he throw things or call you names? Mine used to call me the foulest, most degrading names you can imagine." She grabbed the pitcher and topped off all their glasses. "I'll bet he calls you names."

"No, not the way you mean. He... Really, you'll think I'm being silly."

Vicky gave her hand another squeeze. "Go ahead honey."

"Well, it's the hunting."

"You mean the hunting trips? He's not lying about them so he can have an affair or something, is he?"

"No. I'm sure he really goes hunting."

"They all go hunting," Denise said. "Your father and brothers go hunting. It's just what they do up here."

"I know. It's not the trips. It's... I think it's the killing."

Vicky and Denise looked at one another, then Vicky slid out of the booth and took the empty pitcher to the bar for a refill.

"You know," Denise said, "you have to kill your food to eat it. Unless you're planning on turning vegetarian there's no way to avoid it. You're not, are you?"

"No."

"Well, good. I mean, when you eat a hamburger somebody had to kill the cow."

"I know. It's not that. It's hard to explain." She

shrugged her shoulders, and they sat in silence until Vicky came back with a fresh pitcher and refilled their glasses.

"What are we talking about?"

"Karin's not a vegetarian," Denise said.

"Oh? Well, that's good." Vicky looked at Karin. "So what exactly is the problem? I have to tell you, we like David. He's good-looking and funny, and he went to college."

"Yes," Karin said, "he's very smart."

"And he's good-looking," Denise repeated.

"If the only issue is his hunting trips maybe he'd be willing to cut back on them. At least that's something you can bring up at your counseling sessions. You know, compromise is the key to a happy marriage."

"My ex and I compromised," Denise said. "I suggested he move the hell out, and he did. Now he's compromising some bitch over in Wautoma."

"It's not the hunting trips." Karin took a sip of appletini. "Okay, here's what happened. After his last hunting trip he brought home a doe. He's brought home doe before, and we've had them butchered and eaten them, just like the bucks. This one was different. He had her head mounted. She's hanging on the wall over the pool table."

"Hell, girl," Denise said, "we had dead animals all over the house. Before we got the flat screen there was a mangy-looking bobcat sitting on the TV. The taxidermist tried to give it a snarl, but I always thought it looked confused, like, 'How the hell did I get here?'"

"Does he know it upsets you?" Vicky asked. "Maybe he'd be willing to take it down."

"It's not so much the doe's presence; it's what he did

when he hung her there. He sat in a chair across the room and stared at her for a few minutes, and then he said,

> 'When I all weary had the chase forsook,
> The gentle deer return'd the self-same way,
> Thinking to quench her thirst at the next brook.
> There she beholding me with milder look,
> Sought not to fly, but fearless still did bide:
> Till I in hand her yet half trembling took,
> And with her own goodwill her firmly tied.'"

"Why, that's poetry, probably something he remembered from school. Honey, are you sure he wasn't talking to you?"

Karin tossed back the rest of her drink. "Ladies, he didn't even know I was in the room."

o

Baking was one of the ways Karin tried to connect to her mother. Her mother had taught her how to bake when Karin was in the fourth grade. Today she was baking an apple pie. *From grandmother to mother to me,* she thought. *Decades of apple pie baking, now turned into therapy.*

She floured her board and, for the umpteenth time, was thrilled by the way the cloud of sifted flour spread like smoke. The way it leached the moisture from her hands made her aware that her DNA was being kneaded into the dough. Muscles in her arms and shoulders that she rarely used were brought into play. She had to tell herself, as her mother had, to go easy; pie dough is not bread dough. She tried to imagine what other words of wisdom her mother would have disclosed between slicing the apples and greasing the pans. Her mother didn't bake for Karin's father; she baked for herself. During their baking sessions she had told Karin that it was important to have something that was just yours, something that nurtured emotional independence. She called it her "frigjordhet." Karin was grateful that her mother had shared frigjordhet with her.

The other bit of philosophy that her mother had shared with Karin was, "you are you," meaning pay attention to your own life and your own behavior. "The opinions," she had said, "of your teachers, parents and friends are just that, opinions. You are the one who has to live with your decisions, so use your own judgement." Karin decided to use her own judgement now. Her mother's apple pie recipe called for chopped walnuts. Karin wasn't fond of walnuts, so she left them out. She added more cinnamon as compensation. As she did she thought that, though her mother had been a strong mother, she had been a weak wife. She had remained married to a man with whom she had very little in common long after they had stopped enjoying one another's company. Karin's parents were an attractive couple who had attractive children. They were active and well-liked, and the people who knew them socially would never have guessed that they often went several weeks without speaking.

Karin slid the pie into the oven, tossed her apron on the counter, and went out to the living room. She slumped into a chair across from the mounted doe's head and stared up at it while she waited for the fragrance of the pie to drift out from the kitchen and find her. She knew the power of that smell; butter, apple, sugar and cinnamon melting together— the smell of frigjordhet.

o

Karin told herself that during their next appointment with Dr. Paretta she'd try to keep an open mind. She appreciated her friends telling her they had thought she and David were a perfect couple. On their first date someone had mentioned how good they looked together, and she had thought so, too. Halfway though the session, though, she started feeling pressured.

"If you could change one thing about your marriage, what would it be?" Dr. Paretta asked.

Karin thought about it. What could David possibly do that would change the way she felt? What could she do?

"Nothing," she said.

o

She had hoped to be packed and gone before David got home from work, but as she carried her suitcases from the bedroom she heard his car crunching up the gravel drive. She opened the front door and lugged her bags out to her car, afraid to break her momentum, afraid of losing her resolve. She managed to get the bags loaded and was in the driver's seat when he tapped on her window. She lowered the window but continued to look straight ahead. For a minute neither of them spoke. She could sense his anxiety. Finally, she turned and, for the first time in weeks, looked him in the face.

"Why?" he asked.

She knew whatever she told him would be inadequate. She knew there was nothing she could say that would really explain "why." She gave him the only explanation she could think of.

"We each wrote our own wedding vows," she said. "I know it's been a long time since that day, but I can still see us, facing one another in the front of the church. I was nervous and my hands were shaking and my palms were slick with persperation. You held both my hands; your firm grip quieting my nerves. You looked into my eyes and recited an old poem by Edmund Spenser. Do you remember it?" Before he could speak, she continued. "I remember it. At the time I was thrilled.

> 'When I all weary had the chase forsook,
> The gentle deer return'd the self-same way,
> Thinking to quench her thirst at the next brook.
> There she beholding me with milder look,
> Sought not to fly, but fearless still did bide:
> Till I in hand her yet half trembling took,
> And with her own goodwill her firmly tied.'"

Karin backed her car down the driveway and, without looking back, was gone.

SECRET GARDEN

The woods were foreign to Ben. The uneven ground upset his balance, and as he ran he caught his boots on roots and rocks, stumbling, getting up and stumbling again. Branches whipped across his face, stinging, blinding him. He had left the path to elude the two teenage boys who were chasing him, but he was making too much noise. He paused a moment to rest, his back against a tall tree, and listened. A cloud of mosquitoes found him, but over the hum he could hear the boys shouting to one another as they ran, one of them calling his name and whooping. "Ben! C'mon, old man, whooo! We got ya!"

They were close, Ben thought, and they'd split up, trying to flank him. He ran on, moving away from the shouting. He wiped his face with the grimy sleeve of his pea coat and panicked when he saw the red, his face bleeding from a half dozen small cuts.

"Yo, Ben!" One of them was on his left. He could see movement through the foliage, something blue behind all the green. He cut right, zigzagging now in an effort to keep the trees between himself and his pursuer. Suddenly the branches parted, and he was in a small clearing. He didn't like being out in the open, but he couldn't turn back. He stooped low and moved off to his right, wading through the tall grass, hoping to double back and find some place to hide. A rock turned under his foot and he fell, catching himself on hands and knees. When he looked up he saw one of the boys standing in the middle of the clearing, whistling and waving at someone behind him. Ben turned and saw the other boy, the one who had shouted, emerge from the woods, smiling and fitting a hunting bolt onto the flight rail of a crossbow. Ben stood and faced the boy, holding his arms out, pleading. An arrow flew from behind and pierced his right forearm. Ben screamed. He turned toward the boy who had shot him and saw him place the end of his crossbow on the ground, put his foot into the metal stirrup and bend to grip the string. Ben started to run until another bolt chunked into his thigh. This time he went down hard, pushed himself to his knees and started to crawl. Through the roaring in his ears he heard the click of the first boy's cocking mechanism as he pulled the bowstring into place. The boys took turns, one fired while the other loaded and so on. They kept firing long after Ben was dead.

o

Music blared from the car radio as Mary inched through traffic, but she wasn't really listening. She was thinking about the walls of her cubicle. They were the color of cream of broccoli soup. Depressing. She would probably have canned soup for lunch, but the question was where—desk or diner? She hated eating at her desk, and it only took a few minutes to drive to the diner. The diner soup tasted like it was canned too. Probably came from a fifty-five gallon drum.

She was thinking about soup when smoke began streaming from under the hood of her car. She pulled onto the shoulder and switched off the engine. The smoke was thick, and it was swirling around the car like cream poured into a glass of iced coffee. She took her suit coat and purse and walked up the embankment to watch it. The smell of burning plastic reminded her of the new carpet fumes at her office. Both odors nauseated her. She considered the possibility that the car might explode, like on TV, and she thought that would be cool. She wasn't even upset. She didn't care if she got to work or not. She looked around and saw an oak near a clump of bushes, walked over, and sat in the shade under the tree. In fact, she didn't care if she ever got to work. "Why bother," she said out loud. "I sell crap to people so I can make enough money to buy the crap someone else is trying to sell to me. The company can easily swap me out for some other widget."

She took out her cell phone, and called her husband.

"Jeffrey, my car's on fire."

"Holy shit!" he said. "Are you okay?"

"Better than okay," she said. "I've had a revelation."

Just then the gas tank ruptured. There was no explosion, but the spreading gasoline caught fire, and flames shot up into the morning sky. The car was engulfed in black smoke.

She couldn't explain why she wasn't coming home, and having to come up with a reason frustrated her, so she threw her phone into the burning car. He must have tried to call her back because she could hear her ring tone for a minute before the phone melted. She smiled, thinking about how irritated Jeffrey must be. He was a man for whom everything had come easily. Tall, with great hair and a prominent jaw line, his ascent from copywriter to managing director to vice president had been swift and sure. She could have made creative director, they worked at the same company, but after they married she realized that working for her husband would kill the marriage, so she went to another firm. Jeffrey was annoyingly smug in his effortless success, but Jeffrey wasn't the problem. She didn't want to go to work, and she didn't want to go home, and she didn't know why. Then she remembered the grocery store.

There's a TV in the checkout line that plays commercials for products the store sells. One day last week, she had gotten in line and the TV was showing a commercial for cereal. She watched it for a second, then left the line and went to the cereal aisle. When she got back in line there was a commercial for baked beans playing. She turned around and, even though she doesn't like baked beans, went to get some. After she paid, the clerk handed her some coupons for other products she might want to purchase. The coupons had been selected by a computer based on her previous buying habits. *I don't want a computer analyzing my purchases*, she thought, *and I certainly don't want to watch commercials on screens above checkout lines or gas pumps or read the framed ads in the stalls of public washrooms. I don't want to be told how to dress or what to buy or that I'm too fat or too old. I don't want to be a consumer.*

o

She started with a little tent in the bushes, but soon she had to move further into the woods. People could see her camp from the highway, and one morning she saw a cop car pull onto the shoulder. Jeffrey had brought her the tent, along with some cans of soup. *He was really being very good about the whole thing,* she thought. The girls were pretty much on their own, the youngest away at college, and Jeffrey spent most of their time together glued to the television. With the kids gone they didn't have a lot to talk about, and sex had become a perfunctory activity for them. Being post-menopausal was a liberating experience for her, but she knew that her lack of interest was difficult for Jeffrey. She used to wish he would find a mistress until it dawned on her that television had become his mistress. His ad sense would kick in during the commercials, and he often critiqued them out loud.

For a while Jeffrey came to see her every day, then once a week, then less. He always brought soup, though. The last time she saw him he gave her two cases of corn chowder.

"You'll like this. It's a thick soup with a nice texture, southwestern style, so there's a little zing to it."

"Thanks," she said.

He stood there, holding the case of soup, looking for a place to set it down. "Some reporters came by. They heard about you and wanted to know why you were living out here."

"Did you tell them?" she asked.

"How could I? I don't understand it, either. He set the soup down and went back to his car for the second case.

Mary opened the first box and pulled out a can. It was a more expensive soup than the others he had brought. Jeffrey wasn't cheap, exactly, but he wasn't the sort of person to splurge on soup. This was his way of cleansing his conscience.

Mary knew he wouldn't be back.

Colin unscrewed the barbed head of the hunting arrow, pushed the shaft back out of the hole in the man's neck, and tossed the two parts into an open backpack. He paused to watch his friend struggling with the arrow in the man's calf.

"This thing is stuck tight, must've hit bone."

"Try pushing it all the way through, Dick." He handed him a large, flat-faced rock. "You can borrow my hammer."

The two sat in the middle of a clearing surrounded by woods on three sides and a river on the fourth. Unlike their dark-haired victim, both were blond. They wore baggy, madras plaid shorts and 'crombie t-shirts. Dick was over six feet tall and gangly and felt uncomfortable sitting on the ground. He showed it by continually slapping imaginary insects off his legs. "Did you get our hundred dollar bill back?" he asked.

"Yeah," Colin said, "it was in his coat pocket along with his VA card and some other junk. You'd think these old bums would be a bit more cautious about why some stranger wants to give them a hundred bucks. I guess we can think of this as a cautionary tale about the dangers of alcohol consumption."

"Why do we have to take the arrows with us, anyway? We should just bury these human pincushions the way they are." Dick looked around the clearing. A shallow grave waited next to the corpse and mounds of overturned earth marked the three graves containing their previous victims. "Besides, this is taking too long. It's giving me the creeps."

"Relax," Colin said. "We're fine. No one ever comes out here. And we have to take the arrows because, if the bodies are found, we don't want the cops looking for guys with crossbows. Without these bolts our chubby friend here could just as easily have been shot with an arrow from a hunting bow. Besides, they're expensive." He crawled over to the grave and shoveled a little more dirt out with his entrenching tool. "Looks like he's going to need more room. That was a nice shot, by the way."

"What, through the calf? Thanks." He chuckled. "Dude went down like a water buffalo."

"That reminds me," Colin said, "you ever have a heel spur?"

"What? Hell, no. What is it?"

"It's a pain, starts in your heel and moves up your leg. I think I got it from track practice. I could barely keep up with this lard ass, today."

Dick gave the arrow another whack with the rock and the barbed head popped out of the corpse's shin. "Ah, that got it. Nope, never had a heel spur. What do you take for it?" He sat back and set his feet on the corpse's hip and shoulder, then shoved him into the grave. Colin started to cover him with dirt.

"I dunno," he said, "but I've got to find something. It's fuckin' killing me."

They gathered up their crossbows and backpacks and started the long hike back through the woods. Colin winced with each limping step.

o

Mary gave up the tent when the people showed up. By that time Maize had come to stay with her. Maize was the biggest cat she'd ever seen, brown with white patches and missing part of his tail and part of an ear, and the only cat she'd ever known who liked corn chowder. That's why she named him Maize. Like the Indian word, she thought. Maize wouldn't let Mary pet him, but at night he slept pressed against her back for warmth. Mary liked the way he felt, all firm and muscly but kind of soft at the same time.

They moved to a spot behind an abandoned factory when the crowds got too thick. Most of them were people who had heard about her on TV. Some were homeless or had lost their jobs. Some had substance abuse problems or were just plain nuts, but some were dropouts, like her. They just started showing up, setting up their tents and making a lot of noise. Some of them tried to make friends, but Mary wasn't interested. The last time she counted, there were over a hundred of them, and they just kept coming. Someone nicknamed her "Lady Luddite," a name that thrilled the news media. A local television reporter cajoled her into an interview. She tried to explain that she had nothing against technology per se; what she objected to was the way it was being used to turn human beings into commodities. The reporter ended the interview with, "And there you have it. Words of wisdom from the woman who hates society, Lady Luddite."

She gave a woman with a little girl her tent before she left. The girl called Maize "Kitkit" and kept trying to pick him up. "Why the hell would you let your daughter play with a feral cat?" Mary asked the woman. "The kid's lucky Maize didn't take her eye out." She and Maize were both glad to leave.

They set up housekeeping in a lean-to made of wood pallets covered with plastic. She stacked them against the back wall of an abandoned factory for support. There was a big, overgrown field behind the factory where the railroad tracks and the loading platforms used to be. The walls were covered with gang graffiti, but she wasn't worried. Gangs didn't care about crazy, cat ladies. On the other side of the field was a forest preserve.

It was Maize who helped her learn to hunt and forage. One day Mary found a dead rodent in front of the lean-to. She thought it was a vole. It looked kind of like a mouse, but its eyes were small for its face and it had a pointier nose. It would have been beautiful except for its long claws. Maize had killed it and brought it home. Mary stroked the little animal with her thumb, admiring its soft, velvety fur, then stashed it under an overturned pot. That night she skinned it and added it to some tomato soup to make a little vole stew. She had long ago run out of corn chowder.

After that she spent a good part of every day roaming the forest preserve, collecting edible plants and filling jugs with water from the little river that bisected the preserve. She quickly learned to boil the water before drinking it, and she only ate plants she knew were non-poisonous. Even then, the taste took some getting used to. Some days she wouldn't find much of anything, but she never worried. She loved foraging, and she loved swimming. She had spent most of her teenage summers at her family's lakefront, Wisconsin cabin. Her parents would probably have said she was an introvert, but she liked to think of herself as independent. She would leave the cabin early, before anyone was up, and march into the woods with a swimsuit, towel, and a few sandwiches in a bag, not returning until dinnertime. Her explorations involved climbing trees, hiking off-trail, wading through streams, and swimming in the lake. She collected milkweed pods with their fluffy contents bursting out and cast off cicada shells, awed that the split skin retained all the detail of the insect. One summer she found a secluded meadow with a pixie ring, a circle of mushrooms, growing in it. This quickly became her favorite spot, and she would spend hours there, daydreaming and singing made-up songs. She thought of it as her secret garden.

Thirty-five years later, her body was remembering. She shed layers of fat and her skin quickly colored under the late-summer sun. Her hair, no longer dyed, was streaked with grey, and it rippled as she sliced through the water, flowing dolphin-like, her cupped hands pulling her forward. Now, her explorations had purpose. She collected cattail shoots and water lilies. She hunted frogs at dusk and snuck up on turtles sunning themselves at midday. At first her catch was small, but soon she learned how to lead them, anticipating timing and direction. The frogs tasted better, but the turtles were easier to catch. Most turtles dived straight down before making the run to the dark water under the riverbank's overhang.

o

She was lounging in the late afternoon sun on a mossy patch of riverbank after a day of fishing. She was drunk on the musty smell of the river mixed with the pine of the surrounding trees, and she opened her lungs to suck in the air. Her pronged gigging stick and a mesh bag with her catch, two large turtles and half a dozen bluegill, lay nearby. Maize slept at her feet. *Who knew cats could snore*, she thought. A cool breeze raised a few goose bumps on her bare skin, making her aware of her body. Her flat stomach and muscled thighs amazed her. At fifty, she was in the best shape of her life. She started to think of all the diets she'd tried, but stopped. Thinking about her civilized self made her melancholy. She had no desire to go back, but she missed her children. "They must think I'm crazy," she said. Then she remembered the last time they had all been together, Jeffrey watching television and the girls constantly texting their friends—all of them together but not together. She wished she could explain her self-imposed exile to them, but she knew they wouldn't understand. They were glad participants in a system that cared more about their pocketbooks than their humanity.

Maize heard the noise first. Instantly awake, his ears turned toward the sound, and he shifted his weight onto his haunches, ready to run. Mary moved behind a tree and pulled on her shorts, t-shirt and sneakers. People were coming toward them, running through the woods and shouting. Mary considered climbing a tree to get a look at them but rejected the idea. She didn't want to be stuck in a tree if they spotted her. She grabbed her catch bag and bent low, moving along the riverbank until she found a mound of dirt covered with prairie grass. She lay on her stomach and inched forward through the grass to get a view of the clearing. She hissed at Maize to follow her, but the cat stayed where he was.

Someone emerged from the woods across the clearing, just opposite Mary's hiding place. A man, she thought, and he carried something that looked like a short rifle. He knelt beside a log at the edge of the clearing and raised the rifle to his shoulder. Another man came into the clearing about twenty feet to the left of the first man. This one ran hunched over, holding his stomach. A third man stepped into the clearing on the same path as the running man. He carried a short rifle, too. The running man was coming toward her when he suddenly stood, arching his body as though something had struck him in the back and then pitched forward to disappear into the tall grass. The wind rippled the grass in her direction, like waves on an ocean, carrying with it the sound of the fallen man's crying.

At first she thought the man had tripped. There had been no shot, no report from the rifles. The two standing men walked to where the other man lay, and she could see that they were no older than her youngest daughter. They pointed their rifles down. This time Mary heard the twang of the bowstrings, and the fallen man stopped crying. She pressed her forehead into the dirt and closed her eyes. Civilization had found her, and it had brought murder with it.

She backed down the way she had come and was about to cross the river to the woods on the other side when she saw Maize, standing in a crouch, his ears flat against his head and one of the men moving toward him, fitting an arrow into his crossbow.

"Hey Colin," the man shouted over his shoulder, "I'll bet you five bucks I can get this cat with one shot."

"Leave it alone, Dick," Colin said, "and help me de-arrow this guy. He smells like beer and piss."

Dick ignored him and lay on his stomach, adjusting the telescopic sight on his crossbow as he aimed at Maize. Mary started to panic. She hissed at the cat, but he ignored her. She picked up a rock with the intention of spoiling the man's shot but realized that he was too far away. She didn't trust her aim. In frustration, she stood and threw the rock at Maize. The cat was so wound up that he leaped into the air, then ran up the nearest tree. Dick tried to get a bead on him, but he was used to larger targets. The arrow thunked harmlessly into the base of the tree.

Mary tried to duck back into the tall grass, but it was too late. Dick had spotted her, and he was scared. "Colin!" he shouted. "We've got a witness—a goddamned witness!"

Mary watched, unable to move, as Dick cocked the crossbow, putting his foot in the stirrup and pulling back the string. She wanted to run, to get across the river, but she had seen the speed and power of the arrow he fired at Maize. She imagined being hit as she swam, her blood swirling, mixing with the water, the current piloting her lifeless body downstream. The string clicked into place, and Dick reached to pull an arrow from the quiver on his belt. Mary started to run. She didn't run away but ran straight at him, screaming, a forest banshee trailing the mesh bag behind her. The sight startled him, slowing him just long enough for Mary to reach him. Before Dick could load his weapon she was in front of him, swinging the mesh bag up from the ground with all the power of her anger and fear. The bag split open as the turtles cracked him on the side of his head, and he fell back, the arrow slipping from his fingers. He looked up at her from his seat among the spilled fish.

"You crazy bitch!" he shouted. A red welt was growing over his eye, and he rubbed it, then reached for the fallen arrow. Mary snatched it up and took a step back. She would have run then, but she saw Colin level his crossbow, aiming at her head. "Stay down!" Colin shouted, but Dick ignored him and sprang to his feet, reaching for her just as his friend fired. The arrow slammed into the base of his skull, throwing him forward to clutch at Mary as he fell past her. She stood, staring down at the dying boy until she heard Colin scream. It was a long, sorrowful wail, garbled and unintelligible, but she understood it's meaning as he stumbled toward her, and the cry morphed from pain to rage. Colin raised his crossbow over his head, wielding it like a club, and Mary leapt to meet him. She struck at him with the arrow in her hand, forgetting its lethality, piercing his neck, severing his carotid artery. Without meaning to she had killed the boy.

o

Autumn came quickly to the forest. Mary had spent most of one day hiking to the nearest gas station. The attendant let her use his cell phone, their pay phone having been taken out years before. She called Jeffrey, and when he didn't answer she sent him a text message—*Bring warm clothes and soup please* :-) She added a smiley-face emoticon on a whim. Jeffrey brought her a carload of supplies and worried letters from their daughters, imploring her to come home. Instead, she and Maize abandoned the pallet lean-to and moved deeper into the woods. She had kept Colin's entrenching tool after using it to bury the two boys in the clearing, and she used it to dig a wide pit over which she constructed a dome of branches and vinyl-coated, nylon tarps. She left a hole in the center, like the ones she had seen in yurts and teepees, which she could open or close for ventilation, allowing her to have small, indoor fires on cold nights.

She had buried the boys so that their graves, along

with the graves of their victims, formed a circle, and she visited the clearing at least once a week. She didn't mourn the boys, though she felt bad for the men they had killed. She went there because it was a peaceful place. Sometimes she would sit silently, watching Maize stalk field mice in the tall grass, and sometimes she would nap in the afternoon sun. She often thought of it as a holy place. In the winter she came just to marvel at the way the shadows curved and stretched across the snow-covered mounds, and in the spring she planted choruses of wildflowers on the graves.

A SOFT PERSISTENT RAIN

Florence was going to the laundry room when she stumbled over a cardboard box in front of her apartment door. She almost didn't pick it up.

"Lousy kids," she muttered. "Always leaving their crap in the hall."

There was a sheet of notebook paper taped to the box and she bent down to read it. It read, "Please give me a good home." When she opened the box a green parakeet cocked its head to one side and looked up at her from a bed of torn newspaper. "Chirrrup," it said.

"What the hell is wrong with people, anyway. What makes anyone think I want to take care of their damn bird? I've got better things to do than spend my time cleaning up bird crap, dammit."

She pushed the box inside with her foot, closed the door and continued on to the laundry room.

o

The last stop on the bus line was seven blocks short of home and Florence walked them in the rain. She hated the rain. It reminded her of the day she found out that her son had been killed. She didn't remember much about that day.

Some men had come to the door and given her a medal and a flag. It had been raining the day the men came just like it had been raining in Vietnam the day Robert's helicopter was shot down. No one told her that it had been raining, but she was certain of it. Robert had sent pictures of Vietnam, and in all the pictures it was raining. The medal and flag were still downstairs in her storage space.

As soon as she opened the door the parakeet started chirping.

"Stupid bird," she growled. She dumped an armload of grocery bags on the kitchen table. She shook the rain off her coat, wiped her glasses on a dish towel, and pulled a box from one of the bags. She waggled it at the bird.

"Look what I've got here, dummy—bird food. The kind the pet shop man says you have to have. The pet shop that's two miles away, and I have to take the bus and walk seven blocks in the damn rain to get to."

The parakeet did a little dance. "Chirrup," it said.

o

The parakeet sat on the arm of the couch and ate the corn chip crumbs that Florence put down for it. She absentmindedly broke off small bits for the bird before dipping the rest of the chip in salsa for herself. They were watching a movie on television. At the commercial Florence looked down at the bird. She started to hand him another piece of corn chip when she noticed a long white bird turd.

"Dammit!" Florence said. "You took a crap right on the arm of the sofa. Didn't your people teach you not to crap on the furniture?"

Still grumbling, she picked him up and put him in the

cage she had bought that afternoon.

"You can stay there until you learn some manners, mister."

Florence cleaned the couch and sat down to watch the rest of the movie. She was sure the parakeet's subsequent chirps sounded sad.

o

Florence tried not to think about her husband. He left ten months after they heard about Robert. He said it was too hard to stay because everything, including Florence, reminded him of Robert. It was just as well. Robert was her only child; even his father couldn't share her grief. She also tried not to think about the friends who, one by one, had stopped calling as her relentless misery drove them away. It was too difficult to be around someone who hated the world; she understood that. She told herself she would have done the same thing. Their families were still whole. They couldn't know what she felt, and she wasn't going to fake happiness. She hated the politicians and the generals. She hated the scientists and the religious leaders. She hated the people who made helicopters and bombs and guns and uniforms. She especially hated the people who bickered, endlessly, about whether or not it had been a good war or a bad war.

One evening she was looking through an album of old family photos, flipping back and forth through the pictures that chronicled Robert's growth. She smiled at his boyish cuteness and chuckled at his adolescent gawkiness. He had rented his prom tuxedo on his own, and the sleeves were too short, the shirt too ruffly. He was still the handsomest boy she had ever seen. She was looking at the photo of ten year-old

Robert with a cast on his arm and remembering the call from the school nurse and the panicky drive to the hospital, when she heard the parakeet cough. The next day she took him to the veterinarian.

"What is it, doc? What's he got?"

The veterinarian turned the squirming bird over in his hand. "It's a fungal infection, I think. We'll take some blood, but I'm pretty sure that's what it is. I'll give you some anti-fungal drops."

"Will it be okay?"

"Most likely. What's the little fellow's name."

"I don't know," she said. Florence was embarrassed. She hadn't given the parakeet a name and she felt negligent. "Someone abandoned him, and I took him in."

"Well," the veterinarian said, "you should call him something."

Florence was flustered. "I don't know what to name him. What about Birdy?"

The veterinarian smiled. "Birdy is a fine name."

o

Florence was sitting on the couch, knitting herself another pair of gloves and watching the latest war news on television. Outside, a soft but persistent rain was falling. The parakeet sat on her shoulder and played with her earring. Bird crap had bleached a speckled pattern into the shoulder of the old t-shirt she wore.

"Ouch. Be careful, Birdy," she said. "Don't hurt mama's ear."

The parakeet cocked its head to one side and chirped.

A CLOSER WALK WITH THEE

James Talcott had learned long ago not to use the clip that fastened his Maglight to the barrel of his shotgun. The idea was to illuminate the enemy, not give them something to shoot at. He held the little flashlight at arm's length, out to one side, as he crept through the brush. He carried the shotgun in his other hand. The Franchi SPAS12 wasn't meant to be held solely by its pistol grip, even with the stock folded over. Fortunately he had strong wrists. Crouching in the mud he glanced up at the near-full moon. If he could keep it between himself and the enemy they wouldn't be able to make his silhouette, and he wouldn't need the flashlight. He doused the light, slipped it into the little pocket on his thigh, and stood up, staying low, careful to keep his knees bent. His black-clad form glided quietly around the perimeter of the clearing, keeping close to the trees.

He could see the enemy ahead, lit by the moon, and he swung the military shotgun up to waist level. There were three of them, two in a group and the third off to the right, about eight feet from the others. He'd take the outsider first, but he'd have to be fast, and accurate. He stepped out into the open and fired at the man on the right, the Franchi bucking in his hand. Sure of his aim, he turned rapidly and fired at the remaining two. He saw one man's face disintegrate; then something pounded him in the chest, knocking him off his feet. He looked for his gun but couldn't find it in the tall grass. He was afraid to look at his chest. He didn't want to know how badly he was wounded; he just wanted to get away. He remembered the body armor he had left at the command post. Damn, damn, damn. He started to crawl.

o

"Hendrix! Get back here!" Sean McKinney tried to make his voice sound stern, but the big poodle was too smart. He turned and barked once, telling them to hurry, then ran down the path. McKinney didn't want to lose sight of the dog, but the little girl at his side was busy studying a black and yellow striped beetle she was balancing on a leaf. He wasn't really worried. There wasn't likely to be anyone else in this part of the forest preserve on a weekday morning; cyclists usually took the wide path by the river. Still, he felt a little uncomfortable when he saw the shaggy, black tail disappear around a bend. The little girl held her leaf up. "Look, Dad. Isn't this a Leptino... Leptino..."

"A Leptinotarsa decemlineata," McKinney said. "Yep, a Colorado beetle, pretty, but very dangerous to crops, especially potatoes. Why you want to learn the Latin names of these insects is beyond me. They're a mouthful of gobbledygook."

She rotated her hand to keep the beetle upright as it crawled along the leaf's edge. "I just think it's interesting," she said.

The dog's urgent barking drifted back to them through the cool, spring air.

"Come on, Bella," McKinney said. "Let's go see what Hendrix is up to."

Instead of McKinney's sandy hair and blue eyes, Angelina had inherited her mother's dark hair and olive skin. McKinney called her Bella because, on the day she was born, he knew that she was the most beautiful thing he had ever seen or would ever see again. Looking at her now, ten years later, he still felt like he was viewing a miracle.

She touched her leaf to a bush and let the beetle crawl across, then took her father's hand. They strolled down the green-canopied path toward the barking dog.

"Just a bowl of butterbeans," McKinney sang. "Pass the cornbread if you please. I don't want no collard greens. Just a bowl of good ol' butter beans!"

"What is that horrible noise you're making, Dad?"

"It's called singing, wise guy. You've heard me sing before."

"Yeah, but this is worse than usual. What's the song?"

"It's a parody of an old hymn, 'A Closer Walk With Thee.' I learned it from my zoology teacher, Professor Boyd. You met him once. Your mother and I had him over for dinner."

"It's too bad Mom couldn't come with us." This is such a perfect spring day. It even smells like spring." It had rained two days earlier, and the air was filled with the scent of damp undergrowth and fresh chlorophyll. She pointed into the woods, to a patch of yellow and blue. "Look, there are flowers, already." Her voice quavered a little.

McKinney looked at her sun-dappled face and sighed. He gave her hand a little squeeze. "Your mom wanted to come with, but she needs to rest. We'll pick some flowers to take her on the way back to the car."

As they rounded the bend, the big black dog came bounding toward them. He barked once, and turned to run back down the path. He stopped in front of something large on the ground. As they got closer McKinney realized it was a man, lying face down across the path. He released his daughter's hand. "Stay here," he said and advanced toward the dog.

Hendrix had stopped barking and was close to the man, head down, growling. McKinney stopped and pointed to the ground at his feet. "Hendrix, front!" he said. On command, the dog trotted over and sat where he had pointed. McKinney dug around in his pocket for a dog treat, offered it to the dog, and snapped on his leash. He handed the leash end to his daughter. "Hang on to this for me, Bella." He scanned the path in front of him and approached the prone figure slowly, taking care not to step on any footprints.

The man lay face down with the shapeless appearance bodies get when there's no longer any muscle tension to give them form, like a water balloon or a half-filled bag of leaves. The face was smeared with some kind of dark grease but the skin that shone through was bone white. He knelt and put two fingers to the side of the man's neck. No pulse. The body was cold, but it didn't smell as bad as most of the corpses McKinney had seen. The man was dressed in black military fatigues with black leather boots and gloves. A dark stain, possibly blood, had seeped out from underneath him and soaked into the dirt.

McKinney looked around. The path was covered with footprints, some new, most old. Only one set, though, came from the woods beyond the body, and McKinney could see reddish splotches along the trail. He bent over the body to look at the liquid that had pooled beneath it. It was definitely blood. He could just make out the torn shirt and the jagged edges of a wound. He didn't want to roll the man over to expose the wound, but he could see a clump of blowfly eggs in the blood on the ground. He took a pencil out of his pocket and used the eraser tip to pull the man's eyelid away from the eye. A small raft of eggs had been laid there, too. If they were from the first flies to arrive the man had probably died fairly recently. Depending on the air temperature, maybe within hours. McKinney would ask the crime scene techs to collect the eggs. He looked at the bottoms of the black leather boots and stood up. He was moving around the dead man to get a look at the footprints coming from the woods when he heard the scuffle of feet on the path behind him.

"No, Hendrix! Stay here! Dad, Hendrix wants to go with you. I don't think I can hold him."

Angelina was struggling to hang on to the excited dog. McKinney turned and walked back down the path. He was here as a father today, not as a criminalist. He would walk Angelina and Hendrix back to the car and use his cell phone to call the police. They were only about ten minutes from the parking lot. He wasn't sure if Schiller Woods was within Chicago's city limits, but he'd call the Chicago Police

Department anyway. He knew some of the detectives who worked the northwest side. He was curious about where the man had come from and how he'd been killed. He took the leash and put his arm around his daughter's shoulder. "Come on, Bella. Let's head back to the car."

The girl looked up at him. "Is that man dead?" she asked. McKinney nodded. They turned and walked in silence back to the car. When they passed the little grove of wildflowers, neither stopped. The only sounds were the wind in the trees and the dog, sniffing through the weeds growing alongside the path.

o

McKinney kept his hands in his pockets as he watched the crime scene tech bag the last of the guns. He was tempted to help, but he knew it wasn't his place. He had led the police to the corpse in the woods and watched as they took photos and searched the path near the body. When the detective in charge of the scene, Scott Bryson, arrived, McKinney followed him down the blood-spattered trail into a clearing. They had met on McKinney's first day at the Illinois State Police Forensic Science Center and immediately hit it off. Bryson was a transplanted south-side cop whose wardrobe was built around a collection of polyester sport shirts and leather jackets. He spoke out of one side of his mouth because the other side was perpetually chewing on an unlit stogie. Bryson was a thorough investigator who relied on the physical evidence, both for investigative leads and in building a case against a suspect. McKinney enjoyed working with him. He called to him from across the clearing.

"Counting this nasty-looking shotgun," McKinney

said, "that makes six guns. All assault weapons, empty and smelling like they were recently fired."

"That's a Franchi," the detective said. "Semi-auto with a folding stock. Very concealable and it'll fire a round as fast as you can pull the trigger. They've been illegal to import into this country for years." He pointed to a black nylon backpack at his feet. "You oughta see what's in here. This guy had enough ammo to take out a platoon." He looked into the pack. "Nine millimeters, shotgun shells, even a box of fifties."

"Fifty calibers?" McKinney asked. "Those are what snipers use to shoot down airplanes." He looked up at the condensation trails criss-crossing the morning sky. A big jet drew a fresh one as it soared off to the west. "We're not too far from the airport here." He shuddered at the thought.

"I know," Bryson said. "This guy was ready for anything. There's a bottle of energy drink and a handful of protein bars in here, too. And a stack of pictures, just like those." He pointed with his cigar to the circle of trees ringing the little clearing. They were covered with photographs of bearded men wearing turbans, kufis and Afghan pakols on their heads. One wore a kaffiyeh. Most of the photos had bullet holes in them. Some had been turned to confetti by a shotgun blast.

McKinney looked around the clearing. The grass had been trampled down, and near the spot where Bryson found the backpack was a muddy area. Even from across the clearing he could see footprints in the mud. A trail of blood led from there to where he stood. He started to walk toward Bryson when the detective held up his hand.

"Watch where you step, McKinney. The ground is covered with ejected casings. I want all of them collected and matched up to the weapon they were fired from."

"Sure," McKinney said. He knew the procedure and was embarrassed that he had to be reminded. "I don't want to mess anything up. It'd just make my job harder." He turned to go. "I'm heading back. Angelina's waiting in the car, and I don't like to leave her by herself too long."

Bryson waved from across the field. "I'll call you at the lab and let you know what we find," he said.

On his way back down the path McKinney stopped and picked two bunches of wildflowers, one for his wife and one for his daughter. When he got back to the car, he found Hendrix sitting up front, in the passenger's seat and Angelina lying across the seat in the back. Her eyes were closed but he could tell she wasn't asleep by her breathing; it was too irregular. McKinney noticed that her cheek and the back of her hand were damp, as though she had been crying. He slid into the front and twisted around in his seat. "Everything okay back there?" he asked.

Angelina sat up. "How did that man die, Dad?"

"Looks like a gunshot wound, Bella." He hesitated. "Why do you ask?"

"Did someone kill him?"

"We don't know yet," he said. "Change seats with Hendrix, will you? I don't want him riding up front without a seat belt."

She crawled forward between the seats of the little Rav 4 and pushed Hendrix into the back. The dog barked once to register his disapproval, then lay down and started licking his paws. McKinney handed Angelina the two small bunches of wildflowers.

"Here, Bella," he said. "One for you and one for your mother."

She held them in her lap as they drove home, not speaking, looking out the window.

o

McKinney was sitting at his desk in the Trace Evidence Unit, writing up a report on his analysis of some paint chips found at the scene of a hit and run, when he finally got a call from Scott Bryson. The detective wanted to know what he had learned from the evidence that had been collected in the woods, and McKinney was ready for him. In addition to the victim's clothing he had analyzed the microscopic material that had been collected from the man's gloves and shirtsleeves. It was gunshot residue with a high concentration of particles containing the right combination of barium, lead, and antimony. McKinney had allowed the fly eggs to mature and checked the weather service for the temperature that night. As he had guessed, the man probably died several hours before he found him on the path. McKinney also collected a number of hairs and fibers from the victim's clothing, but without a suspect there was nothing to compare them to. He had compared the soles of the man's shoes to the shoeprint casts that had been taken at the scene and all the useful prints in the clearing had belonged to the victim.

"It looks to me," McKinney said, "like the guy was all alone out there, at least in the clearing. Maybe he accidentally shot himself."

"That's fine," Bryson said. "But there are a few things

that don't jibe with that theory. I talked to Pulaski in the Firearms Unit before I called you. He tells me there were no shell casings to match the slug the M.E. pulled out of the body. I went over to the morgue and picked it up yesterday. It's a big shotgun slug, a twelve gauge with a plastic wad still attached and some flattened down ridges on the sides that look like they were little fins. I think it's a Brenneke. All of the spent shotgun shells we found were Remington target loads, the kind you use for skeet shooting. They fire little BB shot. The unfired shells in his backpack were the same. None of them could have fired the slug."

"Maybe he was a reloader. You know, picked up his fired shells and put his own charge in them. Maybe he loaded one with a slug, instead of BB shot."

"Could be. But then there's the lack of burnt powder on his shirt. I asked the Firearms Unit to do a distance determination test. I thought maybe he had shot himself, too. They couldn't tell me the distance the slug had been fired from, which means it was probably over twelve feet away."

"So you think someone else was down there?"

"I do," Bryson said. "The guy didn't have any ID on him, but we found his car in the forest preserve parking lot. His name was James Talcott. Delivery driver, early forties, divorced, spent the last eight years living in his mother's basement. She and I talked for over an hour, and then she took me down to see his room. It was filled with stuff about 9/11."

"You mean the terrorist attacks?"

"Yeah, he was obsessed with it. There were three bookcases filled with books and DVDs about the Middle East and posters of Bin Laden and the Twin Towers on all the walls. We brought his computer back here and it was filled with the same stuff. His internet browser had its home page set to one of those forums where people can post their opinions. This one is devoted to discussions of terrorism. Guess what his user name was."

"I don't know, the Lone Ranger?"

"Christian Soldier," Bryson said.

"As in 'onward Christian soldier,' huh. So, was he going to start his own crusade?"

"Uh huh. His mother says he called the basement the 'command post.' She also told me that he hasn't been to church since he was a kid."

"So, you think someone from the forum was in the woods with him."

"Yeah. It could still have been an accidental shooting. Maybe he and a friend were practicing shooting terrorists, and the friend pegged him, got scared, and ran off. I went back out to the woods. There's a deer stand in a tree just outside the clearing. A sniper could have sat up there watching him shoot up those pictures; then—POW! What do you think?"

"I don't know," McKinney said. "Did you find anything in the tree? Any indication that someone was up there?"

"Naw," Bryson admitted. "I just don't see how he could have shot himself from twelve feet away."

o

Even though it was springtime in Chicago, the mornings were cool. McKinney's fleece was zipped up to his chin as he and Hendrix walked the same path they had taken weeks before. The dog didn't seem to mind but the mist that hung in the air had chilled McKinney to the bone. It wasn't too long after sunrise so the chain was still across the entrance to the forest preserve parking lot. Man and dog had walked an additional half-mile from where McKinney parked on Cumberland. He wanted to have one more look around the clearing. The techs had cleaned the area and removed the yellow warning tape, but he wanted to get a look at the deer stand Bryson thought a shooter might have fired from.

When they arrived in the clearing the first thing McKinney noticed was how different it looked. The pictures were gone, the empty cartridges had been picked up, and the flattened down grasses had started to spring back. Nature was claiming her own.

McKinney walked around the glade, looking up at about forty-five degrees. He spotted the deer stand easily. It was just a crotch in a tree, fifteen or twenty feet off the ground. Someone had nailed sections of two by four on the side of the tree as a makeshift ladder. The tree was beyond the clearing's perimeter, and it was obscured from view by a number of branches. It was night when Talcott was there; even so, it seemed strange that he could have failed to notice a person sitting in the deer stand. He found the spot where Talcott was most likely to have been standing. The crime scene photos and his own recollection identified it as having had the most footprints and blood spatters. He wanted to climb up to the deer stand to see if a shooter, sitting in the tree, would have had an unobstructed view of that spot. That's why he brought Hendrix. He would leave the dog in the clearing and climb up to the deer stand with a spotting scope.

He pulled a spiral pet stake out of his pocket and

knelt down to screw it into the ground. The sun was just starting to burn off the haze and as McKinney clipped the dog's leash to the stake he noticed something sparkle in the grass, about five feet to his left. Hendrix licked his cheek and lay down in the grass. McKinney crawled on hands and knees to where he saw the reflected sunlight and pulled the matted grasses apart until he found the source of the reflection, an empty shotgun shell. He looked at the plastic casing. It was a 12 gauge Brenneke KO. If McKinney recalled correctly, the KO had a muzzle velocity of over sixteen hundred feet per second. Quite a recoil compared to the light Remington target loads Bryson had found, and unlike the skeet shot in the Remingtons, the Brenneke fired a heavy slug.

He crawled back to where the dog was lying, took out his spotting scope, and sat. He could see right away that there was a large, twisted tree between him and the deer stand. He looked through the spotting scope and, before he could focus on the deer stand, he saw a knotty growth on the big tree right in front of him, about fifteen feet off the ground. A light patch on the burl showed where a chunk of bark had recently been dislodged. McKinney groaned. He knew he'd have to climb up there to examine it, and he hadn't even had his morning coffee yet.

o

McKinney leaned back against the handmade quilt Catherine had sewn. It was draped across the headboard of their daughter's bed. He struggled to keep his eyes open. It seemed like he was tired all the time lately. Angelina had called to him as he was passing her room and asked him to sit with her. They had stopped reading her bedtime stories two years ago when she had decided she was too old. Lately though, she'd been having a hard time falling asleep. He put an arm around her shoulder. "What's up, Bella?" he asked.

"I keep thinking about that man out in the woods, Dad. Why did he have all those guns?"

"He was just afraid, honey. He was worried that terrorists were going to attack, and he was practicing shooting at them."

"Did someone kill him?" she asked.

"No." McKinney shook his head. "It was an accident."

"Oh." She was quiet for a minute. "We were afraid, too, weren't we? I mean about Mom."

"Yeah," he said. "But we're not afraid anymore, are we? Your mother's going to be fine. She just needs to get a lot of sleep after her chemo and radiation appointments. That's when our bodies do the most healing, when we're asleep."

"I know," Angelina murmured.

He smiled down at her little, shaved head. Its peach fuzz tickled his arm. "You should get to sleep, too. School tomorrow."

"Okay."

Within minutes she was asleep. He slid his arm out from under her and crept out of the room. He stopped as he passed his bedroom and stood for a moment, watching his wife sleep. When he was able to detect the rise and fall of her chest he moved on down the hall to brush his teeth. McKinney looked at his haggard reflection in the bathroom mirror. He thought about James Talcott and his woodland target practice. McKinney had climbed up the gnarled tree and dug out a hunk of the burl with his pocketknife. There was a silvery smear on the wood and elemental analysis with the Scanning Electron Microscope showed that it was of the same lead-heavy composition as the lethal slug. Talcott had accidentally loaded the Brenneke along with his practice shot shells and hadn't been prepared for the extra recoil. It kicked the barrel of the gun skyward and the slug had ricocheted off the hard wood burl, right back down into his chest.

The terrorist attacks on 9/11 had changed the world for James Talcott. The sudden awakening to the possibility of violence and death had made him a victim of the attacks, too. McKinney imagined he had convinced himself that he was just getting everything set, being prepared. Really, McKinney thought, Talcott had been out in the woods that night taking pot shots at his personal demons. He had committed suicide by fear.

McKinney ran his hand over his own recently shaved head, an act of family solidarity Angelina had suggested. They had been lucky. Catherine's mastectomy had taken all the cancer and, for safety, the nearest lymph nodes. It was too early to tell if the disease had spread, but if she made it past the five-year mark...

For a while he and Catherine would laugh a little too loud or a little too long whenever one of them told a joke. They'd try a little too hard to appear relaxed around Angelina, and she, of course, would notice. Eventually, their hair would grow back, and they'd be able to talk about cancer without calling it "the C word." Nothing would ever be the way it was before, though. They too had been touched by fear.

FISH STORY

You can get to know a person pretty well when you're helping him wipe his ass. My name is Ernie Fischetti. I was named after "Mr. Cub," Ernie Banks. I used to hate the Cubs. In fact, until this year, I hated baseball altogether. I hated hearing guys talk about baseball at work or on the train or at parties. I hated listening to pot-bellied, ex-jock sportscasters discuss baseball on TV. I hated baseball hats. I hated… You get the idea.

You may have heard of my father, Charlie Fischetti. He was fairly well known on the North side back in the day. We come from a long line of Chicago Democrats. In fact, my brother was named after hisoner, Mayor Richard J. Daley. That was the first Mayor Daley. In addition to running a print shop my father was a ward heeler. Everybody in the neighborhood knew him, and a few even liked him. He had strong opinions and not much tact. Women, however, found him charming. When he got sick, the women on our block would send food home for him. He never got to taste any of it, though, because my mother would throw it away. She would politely thank Mrs. Koslowski or Mrs. Ramirez or whoever, but she never let them in the house, and as soon as the door was closed she'd march straight to the trash and dump it out. In the months before Charlie died we threw out enough casseroles to feed the whole thirty-third ward.

Charlie's best friend was a guy they called Mookie. He always brought in orders for printed signs from the aldermen and committeemen. Those were the jobs that put me through college. I was the first Fischetti to graduate from a school that didn't offer courses in heating and air conditioning. Mookie was a real character. He was always chomping on a big cigar and every other word out of his mouth was fuck. "Fuck dis" and "fuck dat" and "I oughta stick my big fuckin foot up yer fuckin ass". One year Mookie and my father decided to sponsor a Christmas toy drive for "da poor kids." They shook down every business in the ward, and when they were through they had more toys than FAO Schwarz.

Charlie was good to my mom, who adored him, and he only came home drunk once in a while. One hot July day, on one of their many excursions to Wrigley field, he got the announcer to do him a favor during the seventh inning stretch. I don't know who the announcer was because I refused to go to baseball games with my family. I don't think it was Harry Carry. Anyway, right before singing Take Me Out To the Ball Game whoever it was wished my mom a happy birthday over the PA system. He got the whole crowd to applaud. The best part was that her birthday wasn't until November. Charlie wanted to surprise her.

When I was in grade school Charlie signed me up for Little League. For three summers I spent every Saturday standing out in right field, thinking about bugs. When I was a kid I was crazy about bugs. I knew all their Latin names and which ones were insects and which ones were arachnids. Charlie didn't like bugs. He liked baseball, and he wanted me to like baseball. Whenever the ball was hit out into right field I would miss the catch. Since I wasn't paying attention to the game I would usually throw the ball to the wrong base. The coaches only let me play because they knew Charlie. The other kids wouldn't talk to me. The parents hated me. They would groan whenever I was up to bat. I would occasionally get on first, but more often I would hit a pop up to an infielder or strike out. On Friday nights I would lie awake worrying about the following day's humiliation.

As soon as I hit puberty my interests switched from bugs to girls. My brother could talk baseball with Charlie, but the only balls that interested me were my own and how I could get some girl, any girl, to touch them. When I was in my late twenties my mother started pestering me to get closer to my father. She painted a picture of him as a regretful, middle-aged man who wandered around the house moaning about his poor parenting skills and how he had let Richie and me down when we were kids. We went out on a couple of father/son "bonding" evenings. These were mostly dinners with long, uncomfortable pauses interrupted by an occasional conversation. Sometimes, for variety, we argued over who would pick up the tab.

A typical conversation was, "You know, your namesake, Ernie Banks got the MVP in nineteen fifty eight AND fifty nine, and I saw him play both years. He was one of the greats."

Smile and nod.

"Pitching. It's all about the pitching. If the Cubs had a decent pitching staff they could go all the way this year."

Smile and nod. He just didn't get it. I still hated baseball. I was working as a researcher at the Field Museum of Natural History. I traveled all over the world, evaluating specimens for the permanent collection. I loved my job, and he never asked me one question about it. The most I ever got from him on the topic was, "Still workin' with bugs?"

One time I suggested that we go to the movies. I thought it would eat up a nice chunk of the evening and give us something to talk about over dinner. At the time I was trying to cultivate an interest in "cinema" and the arts so I suggested we see an Andy Warhol film called *Trash* that was screening at a neighborhood art gallery. I guess the title should have been a warning. The film turned out to be the story of a heroin addict who wanders around shooting up and having sex with all kinds of low-life, arty types. This guy's mouth was fouler than Mookie's. Right around the time some pregnant chick started masturbating I realized that I was embarrassed to be watching this movie with my father, and I suggested we go. I was almost happy to sit through his baseball talk over dinner that night.

When Charlie was in his seventies he contracted ALS, a disease that paralyzes its victims. It starts with the extremities and works its way in until the muscles that move your lungs are paralyzed and you stop breathing. It's slow, progressive and incurable. Initially my mother seemed more upset about it than he did. ALS is also known as Lou Gehrig's disease and that's what Charlie called it. He refused to refer to it any other way and, despite Gehrig being a damned Yankee, he seemed to take pride in the idea that he was going to be killed by the same disease that claimed the "Gibraltar in cleats."

He put on a brave face for a few months, but eventually it became obvious that he was depressed. He had shut himself off from all his friends except for Mookie. One day Charlie and Mookie were talking and Mookie was giving him his usual, "You're gonna kick this fuckin disease's ass" pep talk. Charlie joked about how he wished it was diabetes instead so he could be like Ron Santo, the great third baseman on the '69 Cubs. He started to get up to walk to the bathroom and his legs gave out. When he fell Mookie tried to catch him, but he slipped and they both went down. Mookie got up, but when he looked down at Charlie he saw tears in his eyes. Charlie tried to look away, but it was too late. He felt humiliated and Mookie's reassurances only made it worse. After that my mother had instructions to tell Mookie that Charlie was napping whenever he came over. I think it broke Mookie's big, cigar-chomping heart.

One dreary, autumn day I had an argument with my mother. Richie and I had gone over to put up the storm windows and take the air conditioners to the basement. Charlie was depressed and just sat there watching us work without saying a word. Mom started talking about him as though he wasn't there, but he was. He was right there in the room, listening to us talk.

"I can't tell you boys how hard this is. Your father needs something every minute of every day. It's driving me crazy. I can't remember the last time he let me sleep through the night."

"Mom. Shhh."

"Oh, please. Your father's a changed man. He just sits there staring off into space unless he needs something. Then he talks to me like I'm his godam waitress. I'm exhausted."

"But you shouldn't embarrass him by discussing it here. Let's go in the other room if you want to talk."

"What the hell do you know?!" She tossed her dust rag on the floor and stomped out of the room.

Richie and I discussed this later that evening and decided that it wasn't fair that Mom had to bear the brunt of the responsibility for Charlie's care. We were both financially strapped, so having a nurse or caretaker come in was out of the question. We did scrape together enough for a cleaning woman to come twice a month. Finally, Richie came up with an idea that seemed to have multiple benefits. We would take Charlie fishing.

Once, when we were kids, we had all gone fishing on the Des Plaines River. Charlie wanted to show us the spot he used to fish when he was a kid. The water was dirty and polluted. Rusted shopping carts and engine blocks made little islands in the water that were surrounded by swirls of soap scum. We didn't catch a thing, and though Charlie was disappointed at the condition of his old fishing hole, we all had a great time. He even pretended to listen when I told him the names of the bugs we were using for bait.

This was the perfect plan. We would take Charlie somewhere that had actual fish and spend a weekend trying to catch them. Mom would get a well-deserved break, Charlie would get a little taste of fresh air, and Richie and I would have a chance to bond with our father like we had on that childhood fishing trip. Despite his tremors we figured he could still hold a pole. We booked a room and a pontoon boat up in Wisconsin, loaded the trunk with fishing gear and a wheelchair and took off

We had lunch at a little country diner. Fried chicken, mashed potatoes, corn on the cob and a cute, middle-aged waitress who flirted with Charlie through the whole meal. I was cutting the corn off the cob for him when the waitress came by to refill his coffee cup. He looked up at her, his voice choked with embarrassment. "My boys have to help me eat."

She sidled in next to him so that her hip was firm against his shoulder and tousled his hair. "Honey, you're lucky to have boys who love you. My idiot son only calls me when he needs money."

The pontoon boat worked fine. Charlie had been worried that he would fall in the lake and drown, but the boat was stable and we put him in the chair with a seat belt so that, if he hooked into a two hundred pound catfish, he wouldn't be dragged overboard. We stayed out all day without seeing any sign that the lake had ever had a fish in it. We didn't talk much. Richie and I told a few jokes, but Charlie would just nod and smile, kept apart from us by his wall of sadness. That night we ate at a local pub where they assured us that the lake was stocked with enormous bass and walleye. There were a few trophy fish on the walls, and the bartender had a story about each one and the angler who had landed it. Apparently, they were all tough fish who had put up quite a fight. They had worn out the men who caught them, and out in the lake lived their equally vicious cousins, just waiting for the likes of us to hook into them. True fighting fish that would test our mettle and see if we had the right stuff.

We each had a couple of drinks with dinner. Richie and I had discussed this before the trip and decided that it was more important that Charlie have a good time than to be cautious about interactions with his medication.

"I'd like to catch a fish like that," Charlie said. He pointed at an enormous bass with his quivering hand. "But we covered this whole lake today, and I doubt there's a fish left in it."

"Hell," Richie said, "that isn't even a real fish. I bet if you turn it over there's a Made in China sticker on the back."

I raised my glass. "A toast. To fish and waitresses."

Finally Charlie grinned. "You got that right."

"Yeah, she was hot for you," Richie said.

Charlie tossed an ice cube at him. "Don't tease your old man. I'll run you over with my wheelchair."

That night Charlie got up every twenty minutes to go to the bathroom. It wasn't so much that he had to go but that he felt like he had to. He was consistently uncomfortable, and rather than risk crapping his pants he would get up. By that I mean he would get me up. He couldn't get out of bed on his own, so he would lie there and call for help until I woke up and took him to the bathroom. Somehow, Richie managed to sleep through all of this. Granted, his bed was on the other side of the room, but I think he was faking it most of the night. I also found out that when Charlie actually did manage to take a crap he needed help to wipe his ass. He was no longer strong enough to raise his butt off the seat to get his hand back there to wipe. At first I tried to put my hands under his armpits to lift him off the seat, but he was too heavy for me to hold, and that position seemed to shorten his reach. Finally, about four a.m., we came up with the solution.

"You know your mother and I have a technique for this that works pretty good."

"Mom has to hold you up?"

"Sure. Somebody has to."

"Does she get up with you all night long too?"

"I keep the walker by the bed at home. She only has to get up when I need help wiping."

"Okay, what's the technique?"

"I'll bend over, and you put your arms around my middle. Then when you pull me forward I can wipe."

"Sounds good," I said.

He leaned forward at the waist, and I wrapped my arms around him. I found that by rocking back on my heels I could support his weight without too much trouble. I tried not to watch what he was doing, and my gaze fell on the skin on his back. It was almost transparent. It was a yellowish, white color with blue veins and a smattering of dark blotches, and it was thin—thin like wax paper or tissue. It frightened me. I thought, *This is what growing old is.* Then I heard him sob.

"This is hell, Ernie. I'm living in hell. I'm sorry you had to see me this way."

I eased him back onto the seat. "I don't mind, Dad."

"It's humiliating," he said. "I just wish it was over."

We didn't catch any fish the next day either, but we talked more. Richie confided that he and his wife weren't getting along and that they had been going to counseling.

Charlie talked about his will, which made us all uncomfortable, but we were grateful to learn that Mom was well taken care of. I talked about baseball. I asked questions that I didn't even know I knew, and Charlie was glad to have the chance to educate me. He talked about the origin of the designated hitter rule and about the time, in 1998, when Barry Bonds was thrown out after a hit ball bounced off the pitcher's foot. He talked a lot about the Cubs' bullpen, and I didn't mind a bit. Finally, the gentle rocking of the boat and the slap-slap of the waves on the pontoons lulled us into a trance. A kind of easy quiet washed over us.

On the way home Richie had a flash of inspiration. He pulled into a truck stop and told us to wait in the car. When he came back he was carrying three of those big, plastic, singing fish. He tossed one to Charlie and one to me, and then I tossed the third one to Richie. That way we could all say we had caught a fish on our fishing trip. Charlie kept pushing the button on his fish and chuckling. All the way home we were treated to the same twelve bars of *Don't Worry, Be Happy*.

DOWNSIZING

Franklin asked his father why he decided to stop using his arms.

"Well," he said, "after the plant closed I didn't have anything else to do, really. I felt like a tennis racket at a hockey game." He sipped some coffee through a straw. "It's not so bad. At least now I have an excuse for not doing anything."

"But it's not a legitimate excuse," Franklin said.

"Maybe not to you but I'm perfectly happy with it."

He had seen a documentary on cable TV about a man who was paralyzed in a train derailment. The man couldn't use his arms so he taught himself to paint by holding the brush with his toes.

Franklin's mother didn't know what to do. She couldn't just let her husband starve, but she wasn't interested in spoon-feeding him either. Sometimes the food wouldn't make it to his mouth, and it disgusted her to see a grown man with clam chowder on his chin.

"Won't you even feed yourself?" she asked. "All you do is sit around watching television. It's shameful."

"I'm going to learn to paint with my toes," Franklin's father said. "Beautiful paintings of household pets. I'd like to try for the style of John J. Audubon, the famous nineteenth century bird artist."

He began painting watercolor portraits of all of his friends' dogs and cats, holding the brush between his toes. His paintings looked more like a child's drawings of pumpkins or softballs than animals.

Franklin's mother finally had enough and went to stay with her sister in Cincinnati. She said it was creepy to see him walking from room to room with his arms dangling at his sides.

"He looks like one of those zombies," she said.

One night Franklin was channel surfing and ran across a documentary about a paraplegic who traveled around the country giving inspirational talks to people with physical disabilities. It was during dinner, which Franklin's father now ate by lowering his head to the plate like a dog.

"Maybe," Franklin said, "you could travel around the country giving inspirational talks to healthy people who wish they were disabled."

Franklin's father considered it. Franklin pointed out that most people would think it was contemptible, and a few might even take a poke at him.

"I don't know," his father said. "The world's changed. I bet there are lots of folks who'd at least think seriously about trying it."

Franklin thought about it. Then his arms started to feel heavy. His fingers grew numb and clumsy.

"What do you know?" he said.

THE WIND

Schoenhauer walked slowly back from the transport stop down the road. It wasn't far from his house, but the air was hot and dusty, and he was starting to feel his age. He had meant to drop in on his daughter, but their houses were a mile apart and the armload of groceries he carried seemed unusually heavy. Megan met him at the gate and took one of the bags. The wind whipped around him, but he pulled the scarf from his mouth so she could see him smile. They walked around to the kitchen door where he followed her through the membrane and sat down at the table. This was his favorite part of coming home. He and Megan had met the year that his wife died. He had spent three years in the city. He called them his "story years" because they had supplied him with adventures to tell anyone who would take the time to listen, though that was mostly Megan.

Now, she was rummaging through the bags he had brought back from town and attempting to appear casual.

"Oh good, a ripe avocado. I'll use this in the salad tonight. What are these washers for? Is there something wrong with the pump?" She emptied the bags item by item while he squirmed in his chair, trying not to laugh. Finally he couldn't stand it anymore. He pulled a small box out of his overalls and tossed it on the table.

"You're as bad as a kiddo," he said.

She snatched up the box and gave him a look. "And you're a mean old tease. You know I love it when you bring a present." Megan opened the box and took out a small, blue pill. "Tribuzine! Is it this month's?"

Schoenhauer nodded.

"Oh, thank you! I'll take it after dinner." She put the pill back in the box and slipped it in her pocket. Schoenhauer enjoyed making her happy, and she enjoyed letting him. She would have been just as enthusiastic if the box had contained a rock. She listened to his stories, and he brought her little gifts. The symbiotic nature of their relationship was obvious to both of them. If they never talked about love it was because they never had to.

After dinner Megan took the Tribuzine. She sat in her easy chair, her eyes glazed and far away, and tried to describe what she saw.

"There's war in the 51Pegasus outposts again. The Senate wants to tax all nitrogen transports, so it's good we've finally got the waste conversion barn set up. Here comes movie news. Oh dear. Palmer and Stephanie have split up again."

Schoenhauer pushed himself out of his chair and put his coat on.

"I'm off. Goin' over to Ann's," he said. The dominant language on Epsilon7 was English, but Schoenhauer's English was flavored with the thick, rural European of his Earth-born parents.

Megan waved. "Don't stay long. They have their own lives, you know."

Schoenhauer's daughter was just putting away the dinner dishes when she was startled by a knock at the door. The sound of the wind had covered the sound of footsteps. She glanced at the I.D. panel and switched off the barrier, turning the back door membrane from orange to blue.

"Evening Ann."

"Dad."

Schoenhauer sat down at the table. "Is Robert home?"

"He's off at the launch port. Pie?"

Schoenhauer pinched a roll of fat and looked at his protruding stomach. "I could maybe have a little slice. He's not gambling again is he?"

"I don't know, Dad. We've talked about it, but he doesn't seem to be able to quit. He just gets so bored."

Ann set a large piece of pie on the table. Schoenhauer took her hand and held her there so that he could look at her face. He saw fear in her eyes, fear of loss and loneliness.

"It's this place," he said. "It's no good for a young man. There's nothing here but dust and farms and wind. The wind alone could drive you crazy. Meg and me are used to it, but you kids met at college where there was parties and movies and such. You shouldn't be living out here with us old folks."

"I know. Robert wants to move back to Epsilon3, but I don't want to leave you."

"And Meg," he said.

"Yes. And Meg."

She sat in the chair next to him. The texture of his heavy, rough-hewn hand was familiar and reassuring. "We couldn't afford to move now anyway."

"You both have college. I bet you could find good jobs on Epsilon3. Meg took a Tribuzine tonight. I'll ask her to recite the job ads for you tomorrow."

He let go of her hand and picked up his fork, but he had to force himself to eat the pie. Sadness had robbed him of his appetite.

o

Schoenhauer was sitting on a big bag of chicken feed, his shirt drenched in sweat, when Robert entered the barn carrying a thermos of cool beer.

"The women sent me out here with this. God, it's hot in here!"

"Sit and have a drink with me. I want to talk a little."

"I should get those wind vanes back up but..."

Robert didn't want to talk to Schoenhauer. He wasn't in the mood for another lecture on responsibility, but he sat on a box and opened the beer.

"Robert, I got some money saved up that I was gonna use to buy a new harvester for you and Ann."

"Harvester, eh? That'd be good."

Schoenhauer continued, "But I wonder if maybe that money wouldn't be better spent helping you kids move to the Epsilon3 colony."

"Ann wouldn't go. We've talked about it, but she doesn't want to leave you and Meg."

"I'll talk to Ann. Epsilon3 has all the things you young people like to do. I lived there for a few years myself."

"When you were a line cutter at the old launch port there?"

"Yeah. Cutters made good money back then, and I got free rides on the cargo ships. You and Ann both got college. You could do pretty well if you had a little stake to start you out."

Robert stared sullenly down at a dust beetle burrowing between his feet.

"I owe some guys a little money. I gotta pay them first."

Schoenhauer took a long pull from the thermos so he wouldn't have to look at Robert. He had worried that this might happen, and now he wasn't sure how to handle it. In his whole life he had never once been really afraid of anything, but now he was afraid for Ann. He had to be careful not to blow up at Robert. Nothing would be solved by anger.

"Those guys what run the gambling are dangerous. You don't wanna mess with them. How much?"

"Just a couple hundred. I can sell my scoot to a guy I know."

"All right, but if you need help you come to me. No more gambling now, okay? I guess Ann likes you pretty good, and she'd be sad if you was to get yourself knocked off."

Robert smiled. "All right. You'll talk to her about Epsilon3?"

Schoenhauer tossed him the beer. "Sure."

o

Schoenhauer sat up slowly and strained to hear. The wind was howling outside, but he thought he heard a transport door close. Two of the moons were still up, and the light coming through the window illuminated Megan's face. She was still asleep. In repose her face was characteristic of her make and model. It was when she was awake that the illusion of life was complete. Looking at her, Schoenhauer thought that he was very fortunate. Surely no other simulated companion could be as intelligent or as caring as Megan. He slid out of bed and grabbed his pants off the dresser as he went out of the room.

Down by the road, next to a single seat transport, Robert stood talking to a tall man dressed in shiny black body armor. Schoenhauer waved to them as he approached. Robert looked nervous. Schoenhauer ignored him and focused on the man.

"Some kinda trouble, maybe?"

"Go back to bed, Pops. Bobby and I are almost finished here."

Robert's voice was shaky. "This is the guy I owe the money to."

"Money he doesn't seem to have; do you Bobby?"

"You the gambler, eh. How much does he need?"

The man turned to face Schoenhauer. "He's 700 short."

Schoenhauer took a credit rod from his pocket, input his code, and looked at the man.

"Thanks, Pops. Input eleven, star, three, three." He turned toward Robert. "I still have to..."

Schoenhauer grabbed the shoulder strap on the man's body armor and pulled. The strap broke. His time as a line cutter for a cargo rocket line had given him an intuitive feel for danger, and years of back-breaking farm labor had added muscle to his already stocky frame. Schoenhauer took the man's right hand and squeezed until it opened. The man squealed as the bones in his thumb and index finger broke. A small, green cube fell in the dust. Schoenhauer ground it under his heel. The man stood up and tried to strike Schoenhauer with his good arm. Schoenhauer jerked down on the trapped hand, pulling the man off balance and into his rising elbow. The man collapsed. Schoenhauer peeled the body armor off the gambler, picked him up and stuffed him into the little transport.

"You don't have to do nothing except go home." He tossed the body armor in after the gambler, pushed the homing lever and slammed the door. The transport hummed off into the night.

Robert bent down and looked at the ruins of the green cube. Schoenhauer stopped him before he touched it.

"What is it?"

Schoenhauer poked the green chips with the toe of his boot. Underneath was a small, dead insect with a green and yellow striped body. Slowly, the wind covered it with dust.

"We used to call them paral-worms. They burrow under your skin real quick-like. Their dung paralyzes you. They only live about a month, but while they're alive you don't move. Cargo workers show me how to use them in bar fights."

Robert's face lost its color. In the moonlight he looked as pale as a chicken feather. Schoenhauer slapped him on the back.

"Let's go to bed. Big day tomorrow."

When Schoenhauer got home Megan was up. They

sat at the kitchen table, and he told her what had happened while she rubbed liniment on the cuts left by the body armor strap.

"We got to move those kiddos to Epsilon3. That Robert's not a farmer. He's going to get in more trouble. Maybe get Ann in trouble too. Tomorrow I sell some equipment, get them a little money."

"You'll miss them."

Schoenhauer touched Megan's soft hand to his cheek.

"I'll be okay. I'm not so young as I used to be and I got to see that Ann's happy. Besides," he looked into her eyes and smiled, "I got no reason to squawk." He settled back in his chair. "Y'know, that gambler fella reminds me of the time I helped run cargo back to one of the old 51Pegasus colonies. We had finished unloading, and we was in this bar..."

o

Winter on Epsilon7 was just as hard as summer. Instead of dust the wind blew snow, whipping and whirling it and piling it up in banks along the fence line. Schoenhauer was shoveling out the feed lot for the second time that day. He stopped to catch his breath, and a wave of wistfulness washed over him. He missed Ann and Robert, but they had both found work in the city and were doing fine. Ann had beamed them that morning with the news that he was going to be a grandfather. He was so pleased that he barely noticed the weakness in his arm until he dropped the shovel. He shooed some chickens out of the way and bent over to pick it up. He fell to his knees, and then, like a great ship slowing into the dock, lay on his side in the snow. His last thoughts were of

Megan, and he opened his mouth to call for her.

    Megan had been watching Schoenhauer from the kitchen window, and when he fell she ran out to him. She knew before she touched him that he was gone, but she pulled open his coat and listened to the silence in his chest. She lay next to him and put his arm around her shoulders. She thought about what her life would have been like without his callused hands to give her a little touch or pat or caress. His stories had bonded them as audience and performer. They had been each other's comfort in this wind torn outpost. She couldn't have asked for a better companion, and she knew that she would never want to be with another. Ann was gone and would soon be raising her own child. She was sure that Schoenhauer wouldn't mind. She pried open a small plate in her neck and leaned up to kiss Schoenhauer's frozen cheek. She yanked out the wire that fed current to her brain and pulled Schoenhauer's arm tight around her shoulders. The wind whirled around them, and snow began to pile up against her back.

HERO COMPLEX

    I stand on top of the hill, hurling dirt clods at jerks. I lob big, softball-sized chunks. They're slower than the little stingers John is throwing, but I want Bobbie Freeman and his three friends to see them coming. My job is to keep them from charging. A clod explodes in the soft earth at my feet. I see another coming at my head but move smoothly, just enough to let it whiz past. Years of dodge ball have paid off, and I return fire with confidence. I can taste the blood running from my nose. Bobbie's punch had been a surprise, but I got in a good kick to his kneecap before his buddies joined in.
    John shouts, "Your side!" and I see one of the kids moving up the hill toward us. I scoop up a handful of pebbles and let fly. He covers his face with his arms and scurries back down.
    John yelps beside me. He's taken a hit in the shin. He walks it off and continues throwing. John and I are the same age, but he has a pituitary gland problem which makes him a foot shorter than me. He's my best friend and the toughest kid in the sixth grade. I once saw him run straight up the front of a big kid who called him a name. He

landed three, quick punches before the kid shook him off. John is one tough monkey. He's in this fight because of me, but I don't tell him how much I appreciate him backing me up. I hope he knows. I hope he wants this as much as I do. I hope he wants to be a hero, too.

o

One day, when I was in the fourth grade, my little sister came home in tears because her friends had told her that, since she didn't go to church, she couldn't go to Heaven. The next Sunday my mother dressed us up and dragged us off to Sunday school. I immediately began asking the questions that had been growing in my young brain, the seeds of which had been planted by Stan Lee's comic book heroes. As a child I learned philosophy from Spiderman and the Fantastic Four. I wanted to know about free will and Divine Providence. I wanted to know why God wouldn't choose to destroy all our weapons and change the hearts of evil men. I wanted to know why God would allow innocent children to starve or die in wars. I wanted to know why we exist.

Sunday school, it turned out, was taught by hapless adults who had no answers. They didn't even want to hear the questions. They tried to convince us that all we needed was to know that Jesus loved us, and if we loved him back we could go to Heaven. That was the goal, they said, going to Heaven.

It kind of made life on earth seem pointless. And if you had to love Jesus to get there, what was going to happen to people who lived in the jungle and had never even heard of Him? What the heck kind of God was this anyway? What sick game was He playing?

o

    John and I are locked in battle with Bobbie Freeman and his goons because of a kid named David Kominski. David is one of the retarded kids at our school and everyone calls him "Crinkles." John and I don't call him Crinkles. I don't know why the other kids call him that. He used to be in our class for part of the day, but eventually someone would call him Crinkles, and he'd start crying. The teachers would take him back to the Special Ed room where he'd sit until it was time to go home. The Special Ed teacher was only at our school in the morning, so I don't think there was much for him to do in that room by himself. Now he spends the whole day in the Special Ed room. I guess they've got someone else to teach him in the afternoon, but I don't really know.

    Kominski lives at the end of my block. I never see him out playing with the rest of the kids. The only time I see him, outside of school, is in the morning when John and I are walking to school. I leave my house five minutes early every day so I can go over to John's house and walk to school with him and his two brothers. Bobbie Freeman and his friends walk the same route as us. Most mornings we see David Kominski walking alone. John and I usually leave the sidewalk two blocks before the school and take the shortcut past the creek. To do this we have to cut through the construction area. New houses are going up all over the place.

    One day we decide not to take the shortcut and there's David Kominski, sitting on someone's lawn, bawling his eyes out.

I ask, "What's the matter, Kominski?" and John helps him to his feet.

"Bobbie Freeman," he says. "Pick on me."

After school that day John and I discuss the Kominski problem. I suggest that we bodyguard him on the way to school, and John, reluctantly, agrees. When it comes to playing, John and I have an arrangement. We take turns deciding what we're going to play. John has a wide variety of athletic interests, so when it's his turn we get his brothers and a couple of other kids and play football or baseball or street hockey. When it's my turn to choose we always play the same thing. We go into the woods by the creek and pretend we're super heroes. We climb trees and jump off rocks and swing out over the creek on ropes. If people knew how many times John and I have saved their butts from annihilation at the hands of some super menace we'd be famous all over the world.

The bodyguarding thing works pretty well for a while. We time our morning walk so that we're behind David Kominski. We keep a distance of about fifty feet. The first few times we see Bobbie approach we run up to Kominski and walk on either side of him.

"What gives?" Bobbie asks.

"Take off, Bobbie," I say.

"What are you, Crinkles junior?"

I turn to Kominski. "Just keep walking. No one's going to hurt you."

This technique works okay until Bobbie Freeman gets wise. One day he brings along three of his friends. As they approach Kominski, John and I run forward to flank him.

"Three little Crinkles," Bobbie says. "We've got a surprise for you."

I start to tell him to leave us alone, but as I open my mouth to speak, he pops me in the nose. It hurts like hell, but before he can do it again I kick him in the knee. The other three kids move in, and John takes one to the ground with a leg lift. He jumps to his feet and kicks the kid in the back. Kominski screams and takes off running toward the school. John and I run in the other direction, into a cul de sac of new constructions. We scramble up a hill of black dirt next to the newly poured foundation and fill our hands with ammunition.

o

By the time I entered the fifth grade, my parents were active members of the church and were embroiled in a bitter debate over the role of the church in secular matters. We were a middle-class white family going to a middle-class white church in a middle-class white community. We had it pretty good. My mother, and her allies, thought that the church ought to be doing more to help the struggling poor in America, especially the "Negroes." The other adults were worried that "those people" would move into our community, raising crime rates and lowering property values. They argued that the role of the church was to minister to the spirit. My mother argued that Jesus instructed Christians to feed the hungry and clothe the naked. The minister of the church agreed with Jesus so the congregation sent him packing. They voted him out and a less "liberal" minister was sent.

From time to time my mother would drag us into the city to attend a "Negro" church. This church was hot as hell in the summer and freezing in the winter, but the congregation didn't seem to mind. Ladies in sequined dresses would fan themselves with paper fans that had pictures of Jesus printed on them. People in the pews would shout back at the minister, "Tell it!" or "Amen, brother!" and the music wasn't boring. It sounded a little like rock and roll. It was the only church I didn't doze off in during the sermon. I went to Sunday school there, too, and made some friends. Eventually my mother decided that some of the kids should see what our lives were like, so in the summers a little girl named Cathy would come stay with us for a few weeks. We played games across the front lawns with some of the other kids on my block. I hadn't met John yet, but I had been playing with these other kids for years. I thought that we were all friends, but one by one they stopped playing with me. One day some of the guys knocked me down and stole my bike. That was the day they started calling me "nigger lover." When I asked why the kids were doing this, my parents didn't have any good answers. They said it was because the kids were afraid of Cathy. That didn't make any sense to me. She was a skinny little girl with a big smile and funny looking hair. Nobody would be afraid of her.

Pretty soon we started to find trash on our lawn and broken bottles on our front porch. Someone subscribed us to a bunch of magazines, and a record club sent us an unwanted collection of patriotic albums. Who knew Walter

Brennan could sing? Kids at school stopped talking to me, and the neighbors stopped talking to my parents. The incident that pissed me off, though, was when someone sent my sister an invitation to a non-existent birthday party. She was only six. She had put on her best dress and wrapped the present herself. She came home crying, and she cried all day. The handwriting on the invitation belonged to an adult. My father was so angry that someone would do this to his little girl that, had he found out who the perpetrator was, he would have put him in the hospital. He couldn't stand to see his family being hurt and probably would have preferred that we keep a low profile. My mother, however, was energized by these anti-social acts. The job of the Christian, she would tell us, is to comfort the afflicted and afflict the comfortable.

o

John's mother has grounded him from me for a week. She does this every time we get in hot water, and after our fight with Bobbie and his friends the water's plenty hot. We meet at the corner of Kominski's block so we can continue to bodyguard him. We're a little further back today, about a hundred feet. It's a crisp sunny day and Bobbie Freeman's nowhere in sight. About a block from school Kominski suddenly turns and starts screaming at us.

"Leave me alone! I take care of myself! You NOT my friends!" Then he turns and runs off, arms flailing in the air, crying hysterically.

In the principal's office we're instructed to stay away from David Kominski. He doesn't need or want our help. In the future his mother will be driving him to and from school.

After John's grounding is up we mostly play baseball. Sometimes we go for a hike in the woods, but it's never really my turn to choose what we'll play. This lasts for several weeks until one day, down by the creek, we see some kids with wrist rocket sling shots using ball bearings to kill turtles. I look at John, and for a minute I think he's going to wuss out. He must have seen the look in my eyes because he bends down and picks up a rock, a nice stinger. He grins. I pick up a fallen tree branch, and we tear into them.

o

John moved away at the end of that year. I've had many good friends since then, but none that I'd trust to back me up in a fight the way John did. I never had the chance to tell him what I learned from that experience. I may not have tormented David Kominski by calling him Crinkles, but I never called him David either. He was just Kominski to me, not a boy who was frightened and alone and needed a friend but an opportunity for me to feel good about myself. Motives are as important as actions. It's taken me a little while to figure that out.

ANXIETY

THE GENTLE GRIFT

Jack Dunphy drove his sixteen-year-old fist into the face of the kid who was sitting on him and felt the nose give way under his knuckles. Hot red drops freckled his face, and then the weight was gone from his chest. He got up and ran. He didn't run home. He ran to the tracks that bisected his little hometown and, when a freight train finally slowed at the Willow Street crossing, he scrambled into an empty boxcar. His father had warned him; next time he was caught fighting, it was back to military school. He took his father's warning seriously, but that didn't change the fact that he was five feet nothing and had acne so bad that his face was more pus than skin.

It was dusk when the train rolled past the refinery on the edge of town. The flames dancing on top of the smokestacks seemed significant to him, burning away the waste. He leaned back against the wall of the boxcar and watched the flames recede. The vibrating steel excited his whole skeleton.

o

Jack had spent the last twenty minutes listening to Lenny Disco and hadn't heard anything interesting. He looked at his notes: *put call center number on the top of all* pages – email Janice about copy for cover – check with HR about 401K – dress code (tuck in shirt) – they WILL dock pay for tardiness – tardiness? Who the fuck do they think they are? – sign up sheet for ass-kissing fest in break room. He looked around the room. Every face was dutifully trained on a man who droned on, enthralled with his own voice. Everyone referred to Hank Lenard as Lenny Disco. They called him that (not to his face, of course) for two reasons: 1. all of his clothes were made from one hundred percent synthetic fibers 2. disco sucks. Attendance at these weekly meetings was mandatory and Jack had been an attendee since he started at Lenard and Frey two years before. After the first three or four meetings he devised a little game to make them more entertaining. Every week he asked Lenny Disco a question. These started out being fairly sincere inquiries about the company's outdated business model, but lately they had taken on a surreal tone. He held up his hand.

"Jack?"

"Well Hank, I was just thinking that, due to technological advances in the marketplace, our print catalog hasn't kept pace with our internet marketing. Especially in the area of interactive advertising. We have audio and video product demos and little games on our web site, but all you can do with the print catalog is read it."

A few of the newer employees were looking at Jack now. The rest were staring at their notebooks or looking out the window.

"I'm not sure there's much we can do about that, Jack. After all, print is…"

"Scratch and sniff."

A woman from the call center moaned. Jack's supervisor, David Finney, glared at him.

"We have several products that could really benefit from an olfactory marketing initiative. Just off the top of my head, I'm thinking scented candles and cheese logs."

o

To celebrate his eighteenth birthday Jack decided to treat himself to a jar of pickles from the corner market. He picked up a jar of big dills and waved to the clerk as he strode past the register and out the door. The clerk dashed after him. Jack let him keep pace for awhile, then increased his speed and left him wheezing behind. At the end of the block he took the corner too fast, and the jar of pickles flipped out of his hand and kept on going. He tried to grab it as it sailed away from him, tumbling end over end. It exploded against the curb.

"Motherfucker!" he said.

He looked back up the street. He didn't see the grocery clerk but decided to keep moving, anyway. They might have called the cops. He grabbed two pickles, wiped them on his pants, and walked off. Usually he boosted cheese. It was easy to hide and had plenty of protein. Sometimes he'd buy a soda or something so he wouldn't look suspicious. Once he had stuffed a pepperoni down the front of his pants so the checkout girl would think he was well endowed. The memory made him laugh out loud.

He turned into the alley that ran behind the movie theater. Sometimes there was popcorn in the dumpster. A movement caught his eye and he recognized a familiar red wool cap.

"Littlebit! What's shakin' bro?"

Littlebit slipped something into his pocket and looked up.

"I ain't your brother, kid. Where'd you get the pickle?"

Jack tossed him one of the pickles. "What you got in your pocket, Bit?"

Littlebit took a healthy bite of pickle and pulled out a small silver-colored box. He handed it to Jack.

Jack first met Littlebit on a job. He had been hired to clean the floor of a grocery, and Littlebit was the guy the agency had teamed him with. They moved up and down the aisles in the empty store with Littlebit pushing the scrubbing machine and Jack scraping up gum. Littlebit told Jack that he got his name by being the runt in the foster home where he grew up. There were five older boys living there who would attack the food on the dinner table like they were afraid it was going to get up and run away before they could stuff it in their mouths. The foster mother always yelled at them to "save little bit for the new boy."

Littlebit was old enough to be Jack's father. He told everyone that he lost his leg in Viet Nam, but he had, in fact, lost it to diabetes. Jack first noticed Littlebit's handicap when he bent down to attack a pink wad with his little trowel. He could see the fading footprints on the damp linoleum and the left one was always lighter than the right. Littlebit didn't put as much weight on his prosthetic leg as he did on his real one. His gait looked like it was driven by an elliptical cog.

After an hour or so he had complained that his stump hurt and went to sit down. Jack finished cleaning and waxing the floor by himself, and when he went in the back to yell at him he found Littlebit sleeping on the floor with his leg off and an empty pint of Dewars in his hand. Jack picked up the leg and looked in the socket. It had a sour odor. There was an area hollowed out in the calf that was just the right size for a pint bottle.

Jack lifted the top off the little silver box. It was empty but for a green felt lining.

"What is it?" he asked.

Littlebit scrunched up his face.

"That's a jewel box. Probably held earrings. My old moms used to have one just like it on her dresser." He took the box from Jack and put it away.

Jack knew that in a few days Littlebit would be telling everyone the silver box had belonged to his mother and was his most treasured possession, and he wouldn't be lying. Littlebit always believed his own lies. Jack didn't hold it against him. He thought that the nature of reality was such that if a man truly believed what he was saying it held the same weight whether it was actually true or not. Much of Jack's philosophy was the product of alcohol, marijuana, and beatings from railroad cops and rednecks.

"I got two bucks from a lady down by the library this morning," Littlebit said. "She told me to have a nice day."

Jack put his hand on Littlebit's shoulder.

"C'mon bro. I've got a buck and a half. With your two we can probably get us a jug."

o

Jack was sitting in the park across from the office eating the avocado and cheese sandwich his wife had made for him and watching the geese chase each other back and forth. David Finney sat down on the bench next to him and opened a can of soda.

"Didn't see you at the party, Jack. You okay?"

"Fine. I just had some work to do."

"Well, I think Maureen saved you a piece of cake."

"Thanks."

"What's up with you lately, Jack? You're surly. You don't come to any of the company functions. You ask these cockamamie questions in meetings. I don't get it."

"Nothing's wrong, David. Everything's normal."

"You're not having trouble at home are you? I mean, I don't want to pry, but—"

"Thanks. No. Nothing's wrong at home. Sunny and I are fine." Jack held up his lunch bag. There was a red crayon heart drawn on it. "She packs me a lunch every day. I'm just feeling a little overwhelmed by the cubicle farm. I'll get over it."

"What do you mean?"

"Well, like this birthday cake thing. At least twice a month we all waddle out of our cubicles like fat blind lab rats, exchange tepid greetings, eat snacks, and waddle back."

"We're just trying to boost morale. What would you do instead?"

Jack sighed. David Finney was okay as managers went but he was no genius. Jack imagined that David bragged to his friends about his many contributions to the corporate juggernaut.

That morning Jack had looked at his own hand under the fluorescent lighting in the office and could see his skeleton.

He was becoming transparent. Soon, he thought, he'd just be a shadow. It wasn't right. People weren't meant to live like this. They need to feel the sun on their faces and breathe unfiltered air. They need to use their muscles so they don't atrophy.

He tossed a piece of bread out to the geese. Two of them moved toward it, but a third, the one with the biggest wingspan, ran in honking and flapping and chased them away.

"I don't know, David," he said. "I'm not blaming you. It's my problem. I'm just having a hard time figuring out what to do about it."

"Well, try and tone down the sarcasm a little bit. Hank Lenard isn't an idiot. He knows you're yanking his chain."

"I'm just trying to keep my self-respect intact. Hell, look what they did to Timer Guy."

"Timer Guy?"

"That shmoe from the call center who carries a kitchen timer everywhere he goes. His supervisor makes him carry it to keep track of how long he's been away from his desk. I first heard it in the bathroom. There was a ticking noise coming from one of the stalls. I thought someone had planted a bomb. Turns out it was Timer Guy, timing how long it takes him to shit." Jack tossed another piece of bread out to the geese. This time he aimed for the two geese who had been chased away before. The big goose came barreling in with his head down and chased them into the pond. "Damn."

o

On his first morning at the commune, Jack woke to the smells of pancakes, coffee, and sandalwood incense.

They grabbed him by the nose and pulled him up from the floor, where he had passed out, smoking pot and listening to music, the night before. He had told the vanload of hippies who picked him up north of Santa Cruz that it was his twenty-first birthday. They'd helped him celebrate. The only other person awake now was the girl who was cooking. She was a little plump, with one heavy yellow braid and pink glowing cheeks. Jack poured himself a cup of coffee and sat down to watch her cook.

"Good coffee," he said. "I'm Jack."

She smiled at him. "I'm Sunrise. They call me Sunny."

"That would have been my first guess."

"It used to be Margaret. I changed it."

She handled the pots and pans with a gracefulness that made simple moves erotic, and the incense haze surrounding her caught the rays of the morning sun. Jack was mesmerized.

He had only meant to crash at the commune for a couple of days, but that quickly turned into a week and then a month and then he found his name on the chore sheet. After that he got up with Sunny every morning to watch her cook. She always drew a syrup heart on his pancakes before setting the plate in front of him. After breakfast he'd feed the chickens and the one old sow they had and then go into town with one of the other men who lived at the commune. Jack got a job at a little printing plant in town. The money he brought in went to pay for the things the hippies couldn't make or grow themselves. It was the closest thing he had to family.

One January evening he and Sunny were lying in bed, talking. They had just finished making love, and Sunny used an errant drop of semen to trace a heart on Jack's stomach.

"Do you ever think about what you'd be like if we had never met?" he asked.

"I wouldn't be as happy."

"Thanks. But I mean, what kind of a person you'd be. Would you be kinder, meaner, smarter, dumber? That sort of thing."

"I hadn't thought of it. I think I'd be pretty much the same."

"Not me. I'm definitely kinder. We've only been together a couple of months, and I can feel myself changing. I want to be a better person because I think you're a better person. You care about things."

"So, what if something happened and I wasn't around anymore? Would you change back?"

He thought about Littlebit. The last time he had seen him was in the bum ward at San Francisco General. He was in a diabetic coma. Jack didn't want to die alone.

"All I know is that right now I see the world in a different way than I did before. I always used to feel like I was being cheated out of something. Like I was watching a game of three card monte, and every time I thought I knew where the queen was, the dealer turned up a deuce. The bet was never enough to break me, but I always felt empty. Like I had lost something that I didn't even know I had. Anyway I just wanted to thank you."

She leaned over and kissed him on the nose.

"If you really want to thank me you can come down

to the shelter with me on weekends. We need someone to help out in the pre-school room."

"I don't know," he said. "Kids make me nervous."

Sunny got out of bed and walked to the closet. She rummaged around in the back for a minute and came up with a big cardboard box.

"I think we're about the same size," she said. "You can wear this. The kids will love you. If you get into the character it makes talking to them easier. Plus, if you see them on the street they won't recognize you."

"What the hell is it?"

She grinned. It was a grin that said, I have you now, Jack. She opened the box and pulled out an enormous dog costume. It was black and brown with four sewn-on paws, a ragged tail and floppy ears. She tossed him the head.

"Your name is Diggedy. I suggest you wear groin protection."

o

Jack plopped down in the chair across the desk from David Finney.

"You wanted to see me?"

"Jack, Mr. Lenard asked me to have a talk with you."

"About?"

"About the crazy questions you ask every week. He knows you're fucking with him and he doesn't appreciate it. He wanted to fire you outright, but I went to bat for you and got you one more chance. Just keep your mouth shut. We don't want to hear any more about raffling off an ostrich or National Salami Day. You're a good worker, but Mr. Lenard, and frankly everyone else, is tired of your shenanigans."

"Shenanigans?"

"You're no different from anyone else here, Jack. You think you're special, such a free spirit? It's time to get with the program, Jack. Get with the program or get out. Think about it."

He thought about it. He lay awake half the night thinking about it. He thought about boosting a turkey dinner from the market so he and Littlebit could have Thanksgiving and how his heart felt like it would bust out of his chest as he eluded the cops. He thought about the time he went to sleep in a dark field and woke up in the middle of a herd of buffalo. Guys like Finney and Lenard couldn't understand how trapped he felt because they had never been free. It was like trying to explain the joy of a warm summer breeze to a fish. If you've lived your whole life under water, the concept of air meant nothing to you.

Around three a.m. he slid out of bed and dug his old dog costume out of the hall closet. It was ratty and falling apart with age, but still jaunty. He had worn it to hand out candy two Halloweens ago. He stuffed it into his backpack. He'd shut up all right. He wouldn't say a word. He'd just sit there, listening to Lenny Disco and taking notes, in his Diggedy Dog costume. He set the pack by the door and went silently back to bed.

o

For his thirtieth birthday Sunny gave Jack the one thing he wanted more than anything else—she married him. They had left the commune right after she graduated from college. Jack had struck out at dozens of jobs. He never had any trouble finding work, but after a couple of months a subtle, inner turbulence would start. It would build in him, coursing through his body, looking for release. Eventually Jack would encase the boss' Mercedes in plastic wrap or cover someone's telephone with Vaseline. Finally, Sunny's uncle gave him a job with his mail order company. Sunny began working with Special Needs children at a local grade school. Jack was surprised every morning that Sunny hadn't packed and left while he was sleeping.

The marriage had been a negotiation. Where Jack wanted union, Sunny wanted stability. She had patiently explained that she would not steal food or sleep in a car or live a life without some sense of purpose. If Jack valued her as much as he said then he needed to show her that he could be responsible. They Eco-honeymooned in Costa Rica. On their last night there Jack woke to the sounds of the rain forest and realized that he was alone in the big rattan bed. Moonlight revealed a sliver of Sunny, sitting cross-legged in front of the sliding glass doors. Jack crawled across the room and sat, legs spread, behind her on the floor. He leaned forward and rested his head on her shoulder. Through the glass he could see the rain forest canopy, black and green with violet shadows, blanketed beneath the moon and the cloudless sky.

"We're so lucky," she said. "Not many people will ever see this."

"If they did, they couldn't destroy it," he said. "There should be a law that the CEOs of any companies that consume natural resources have to spend a week in the jungle."

"I'm worried."

"When we get back I'll research some lobbying organizations. There must be something we can do."

"I mean," she said, "I'm worried about us."

Jack froze. "Why are you worried?"

"I worry about everything. I worry about what we'll do if one of us gets sick. I worry about not having any money saved for retirement. I worry about unforeseen emergencies. Mostly, I worry that you don't worry about those things. I worry that you're going to quit your job, again."

He put his hand under her chin and turned her head. He wanted to see her face, but all that was visible was an outline, from eyebrow to chin. Something shimmered on her cheek. He touched it with his thumb.

"You're my family," he said. "I can't lose you. I know I'm not exactly Mister Responsible, but I do my best. What do I have to do to convince you?"

She found him in the dark, pulled him toward her and kissed him.

"It's easy," she said. "Don't lose this job."

o

Jack set his backpack on his desk. He was an hour early and no one else was in yet. Without people to populate it, and the fluorescents off, the cubicle farm seemed more oppressive than usual. He walked to the back of the room to make sure he was alone, then went back to his cubicle. He wanted to get changed before anyone else got there. He took off his coat, threw it on a chair, and unzipped the backpack. On top of the dog costume was a brown paper bag, his lunch. He pulled it out and looked at it. There was a red construction paper heart stapled to the bag.

DANCE LESSON

Peggy knew it wasn't the little bit of champagne she drank that was causing the room to spin. She was very aware of the problems alcohol could cause her by interacting with her medications, so she had been careful not to overdo. Whirling in the center of the dance floor had never made her dizzy before, and she had whirled hundreds, maybe thousands, of times. The difference, she knew, was that she hadn't been on wheels before.

○

For a time it seemed like her daughter might never get married. It wasn't that Vanessa wasn't pretty or smart, she was, but men just didn't warm to her. All through Vanessa's twenties Peggy had comforted her by telling her she was too pretty. "Men are intimidated by your good looks." In Vanessa's thirties she had blamed her intelligence. "Men don't want women who are smarter than they are. They want to be able to show off a little." The truth, she knew, was that Vanessa was dull. Her appearance, though not unattractive, was more clean and orderly than pretty. She managed a dress shop, but she looked like someone you'd put in charge of scheduling trains or buses. Even her movements were precise. She reminded Peggy of a clock, her gears all perfectly meshed and counting down the minutes of her orderly life.

She was surprised when Vanessa told her she was getting married. She was in the kitchen, microwaving some leftover pizza for her dinner, when the phone rang.

"Mom? It's me. Are you sitting down?"

"Of course," she said. What she wanted to say was, *Of course, I'm sitting down. I'm always sitting down. I've been in a fucking wheelchair since your father died.*

"Guess what? Sonny finally popped the question. We're getting married."

She was glad Vanessa hadn't made her guess. She would have guessed dozens of things before guessing that. She would have guessed that her daughter had learned to play mahjong or taken up taxidermy or had been a hostage in a bank robbery long before guessing she was getting married. *Lots of women get married in their forties*, she thought. *Though I bet those are mostly second or third marriages.*

o

She and Vanessa's father had been an attractive couple, and they moved well together on the dance floor. Geof with a G, she called him. She had loved dancing with Geof almost as much as she loved being married to him. They met at a dance club right after the war. He was the one thing in her life that was stable. Her parents had divorced—an unusual and traumatic event back then. It seemed to her like modern couples married with the underlying assumption that they'd divorce in a few years and try again with someone else. She had lost her job when the soldiers came home from overseas. She understood. They needed the jobs, but it made life difficult. She lived with her mother, and they counted on Peggy's income to make ends meet. Geof was her rock. Even when they were dancing, something they did often throughout their marriage, he kept her anchored. It sometimes felt to her like they were standing still while the other dancers, the room, and the floor all swayed around them.

o

    She was sitting at the table reserved for the wedding party and pretending to listen to the chubbier of the three bridesmaids complain for the second time that the seamstress hadn't hemmed her dress properly. She was thinking about the festivities. The bridesmaids had attached a ball and chain to the groom's ankle, and the best man had tied an apron around her daughter's waist. The couple walked like this from table to table, accepting the "good lucks" and "best wishes" of the guests. After that came the money dance. The men lined up in front of her daughter, and one by one they pinned ten and twenty dollar bills to her apron in payment for a dance. If Vanessa was bothered by the symbolism of all this it didn't show. In fact, she sensed that her daughter was enjoying the attention. Peggy and Geof with a G had simply gone to city hall and then to dinner with her mother. Peggy was pleased that her daughter finally found someone, but she didn't understand the rituals. *Love isn't humiliation*, she thought. Then, Vanessa whooshed down on her and wheeled her onto the dance floor.

    "Listen to that music, Mom. You can't sit still. Come dance with us."

She could smell the champagne on Vanessa's breath. The satin bridal gown made crinkly noises as they circled the floor. For a moment the noise reminded her of something—walking over crackling ice on a winter sidewalk or through a pile of dry leaves. Then, she was being passed from person to person, all Vanessa's friends taking turns twirling her around, pushing her wheelchair back and forth. Her eyes were at butt level, and she had to look up to see their faces. There was Sonny, the groom, grinning down at her. She tried to tell him, "Be good to my girl," but the music was too loud and he passed her chair to the next dancer. It was some woman whose name she couldn't recall. She thought they had met at a church function Vanessa had invited her to last year. Next was a man with a full beard and no mustache. She was certain she had never met him before. She would surely have remembered someone who had chosen to grow something so hideous on his face. *He might as well hang a sign around his neck saying, Do Not Kiss Me.* After that her neck started to cramp so that she had to look straight ahead, surrounded by a sea of unidentified groins and backsides.

o

Now someone was twirling her around, faster and faster. She tried to turn but just caught a glimpse of the culprit. It looked like the best man, a friend of Sonny's whose drunken toast had been laced with the F-word and many references to casual sex. She wanted to wave him off but was afraid to release her grip on the arms of the wheelchair. This wasn't fun; it was dizzying and, as the twirling continued, frightening. Even if she wasn't thrown from the chair she would probably get sick. Geof would never have let this happen to her, let her be passed around like an old-lady-party-favor and spun in the middle of a room filled with strangers. She sobbed then. She didn't mean to. She sobbed and said the one word, "Geof," and then the music stopped, and Vanessa was wheeling her back to the table. Peggy picked up her napkin and dabbed at her eyes. Her daughter patted her on the shoulder and, without a word, trotted back out to the dance-floor and to her new husband.

A FLASH OF LIGHTNING

Jeff grimaced as Liu Tsu smashed a rock-hard fist into his chest over and over again. He was pissed. What had been a simple conditioning exercise the day before was now a test of wills. Today Liu Tsu was hitting him full force. Finally Jeff took a step back.
"Ha!" laughed Liu Tsu. "Soft. Like girl."

Jeff rubbed his chest and tried to get his breathing under control. He had made the journey from Chicago to this mountaintop temple in the middle of China to study martial arts with Shi De Jun, an authentic Shaolin master, but for five days now he and three students from Britain had trained with Liu Tsu, the master's teenage disciple. Shi De Jun, apparently, lived down the mountain, in Deng Feng, at his boarding school for Chinese boys whose parents thought they'd be better off learning Shaolin kung fu than farming.

Jeff didn't mind waking at five thirty every morning or training nine hours a day, breaking only to eat the rice and vegetable mixture that the monks cooked up. He didn't mind sleeping on a wooden pallet or squatting over a hole in the floor to crap or bathing standing up with a pan of cold soapy water. What he did mind was having to take instruction from a little sadist.

Liu Tsu waved his hand in a circle, the signal that they were to run laps again, and went to sit in the shade of the giant ginkgo tree that grew in the middle of the temple courtyard. The courtyard filled with the slap-slap of their gym shoes on the flagstones as the foreign students ran in the mid-day heat.

o

Three years earlier Jeff had been sitting at his desk, filling out expense reports, when the phone rang and a police officer told him about the accident. Jillian had been thrown from her car when another driver ran a red light and struck her broadside. She was dead before the ambulance reached the hospital. He thought about the other car leaping out of nowhere, crumpling her little VW bug. He thought about her fragile body lying broken, on the pavement. He thought about her gentle grace—gone, wasted. He thanked the officer for calling. He quit his job the day after the funeral. His wife was dead, there was no longer any point.

For a couple of months he just floated through life. He spent his mornings reading the newspaper and his afternoons at the movies. He had cashed in his 401K, so he didn't need to work. He spent a lot of time in coffee shops. He told concerned friends and family that he was weighing his options. Mostly, he asked himself the same questions, over and over, in his mind. Why did this happen? Did Jillian feel pain or fear before she died? Could I have prevented the accident if I had been there? What do I do now? Why can't I cry?

He couldn't talk to anyone about it. He felt like a

clenched fist. He was angry all the time and was afraid of lashing out at well-wishers. His mother called so often that he finally stopped answering the phone. Whenever he walked anywhere he punched street signs and parking meters as he passed them. Other pedestrians crossed the street to avoid him, but he never noticed. Once a cop yelled at him for punching a No Parking sign. He stuffed his bruised hands into his pockets and went home.

○

Jeff and Lon, the Scot, had been practicing a two-man staff set for three hours now, striking and blocking with the six-foot long poles. The other two students, Chris and Mark, were learning a broadsword form on the opposite side of the courtyard. Lon was struggling to keep up. Jeff was about ten years older than the Brits, but he was in better shape. He had trained every day of the past three years, filling his time and his mind. Lon was panting and had slipped twice on the rough flagstones, once going down to his knees. His blocks were slow, and Jeff had to be careful not to hit him.

"C'mon man," Jeff said. "It's almost dinner time. You can do it."

Liu Tsu shouted at them from his perch in the shade, "No talking. Concentrate."

"Bloody bastard enjoys making us suffer," Lon said.

"No, he's right. Focus. Here I come." Jeff spun the six-foot staff over his head in "Wind Cuts Through Clouds" as he took a step toward Lon. Then he arced it down toward Lon's knee. Lon blocked with the end of his own staff, but his block was weak. Jeff's staff slid past and rapped him on the shin.

"Ow, that motherfuckin' hurts mate!" he shouted. He

hopped around on one foot for a second, then sat down to rub his shin. Jeff planted his staff and slid down its length to sit next to him.

"Sorry," Jeff said. "You okay?"

"Yeah. You know I spent three years in the Black Guard. That's like your Green Beret. I never felt this sore and out of shape back then."

Xing Bo, the interpreter Shi De Jun had hired to stay with them, appeared. "Dinner time," he announced.

Liu Tsu walked past them shaking his head. Lon pushed himself upright with his staff and hobbled after the teenage sifu. The other two Brits sheathed their swords and trotted after them. Jeff scooted back into the shade and pulled his legs into the lotus position. It felt good to be alone.

The afternoon sun, filtering through the giant ginkgo, painted a dappled oblong on the ground. Jeff looked around at the Buddhist statues and the classrooms that framed the courtyard. He could hear the monks finishing their afternoon chants in the prayer hall up the hill. Above the prayer hall, rose the highest peak of the mountain range. Jeff could see the burial pagoda and the little shrine on the top. The air was spiced with smoke from the giant incense burners and pine from the surrounding forest. Tonight, after dinner, while the other students were reading or playing cards, he would go to prayers with the monks. He had asked the Abbot, through Xing Bo, for permission. The Abbot had been reluctant at first. The monks didn't like having the foreign students there. They housed them in separate quarters as a favor to Shi De Jun, but they considered them a nuisance. They also received a percentage of the students' tuition. Teaching kung fu to foreigners could be profitable.

    Jeff explained about Jillian. He told the Abbot that he could no longer live with his anger. He knew that the monks were wise and the Buddha merciful. He wanted to find some peace. The Abbot nodded and Xing Bo volunteered to go with him and translate the prayers.

o

    Jeff was startled awake by the annoying beep of a backup horn. When he opened his eyes he saw the rear end of a garbage truck coming at him. He crawled out from behind a dumpster and stumbled down the alley to the street. He remembered drinking in a bar the night before but didn't know how he had wound up sleeping in an alley. He checked his wallet. Money, license, everything was intact. His mouth tasted fuzzy, and the buttons were torn off his shirt. His face hurt. He leaned against the side of a parked delivery van and looked at his reflection in the side-view mirror. His cheek was swollen, and there was a bruise under his eye. He had been fighting again. He kicked over a garbage can and sat on it with his elbows on his knees, looking down at the pavement. A cockroach scurried out of the scattered trash and ran nervously past his feet.

    The questions that had plagued him immediately after Jillian's death had coalesced into one excruciating question—why can't I cry? He thought he knew the answer and he knew how horrible it was. That's why he couldn't tell anyone. He could never admit the depth of his selfishness to another person. His wife, whom he loved and cherished, had died, and he hated her for it. She had left him alone, and he was frightened and angry. He hated himself for hating her. His grief was an abomination. Sadness lets you cry. Loneliness lets you cry. Hatred just makes you bitter.

He looked up in time to see a police cruiser enter the alley at the other end. He got up and limped down a companionway to the street, coming out in front of a movie theatre. It was past noon and there was a matinee playing. It was a revival theatre and tickets were only two dollars. He pushed a couple of bills at the cashier and went into the theatre. The movie had already started, and he inched his way down front, waiting for his eyes to adjust to the dark.

As he slid into his seat he heard a yell and caught a flash of movement on the screen. Bruce Lee was fighting a man with long hair in front of an audience of saffron robed Buddhist monks. They both wore black trunks and open fingered boxing gloves. The longhaired man tried to kick Bruce Lee in the face, but Lee threw himself backwards, landed on his shoulders, and snapped back up to his feet, punching the man before he knew what hit him. Then he began to dance around the longhaired man like Muhammad Ali, always on his toes, changing direction unexpectedly, and all the while chopping away at the other man's defenses. A kick to the shin, a flurry of punches, a throw, Lee unleashed an arsenal of balletic mayhem that kept his opponent off-guard until, finally, he took him to the ground and locked his elbow joint. The other man grimaced in pain and tapped his hand on the mat to signal his surrender,

Jeff was breathless as he watched the fight. It was the most exciting thing he had ever witnessed. Bruce Lee's grace and style were the equal of Gene Kelly or Michael Jordan, but his power was like nothing he had ever seen before. Violence, he thought, could be beautiful.

There was a kung fu school near his apartment. He signed up for lessons the next day.

○

Jeff and Xing Bo sat on the smooth wooden floor in a small room, part of a circle of monks. The older monks wore long yellow robes, the novices, matching gray cotton pants and jackets, tied at the waist. There were two nuns among the novices. Jeff had never seen women with shaved heads before. In the middle of the circle was a cast iron pot of sand that held several burning sticks of incense. The Abbot spoke to Jeff, and Xing Bo translated.

"We are going to chant the Diamond Cutter sutra for you. I know that you won't understand what we are saying, but the venerable Buddha may allow you to grasp our meaning. While we are chanting, please think on these words—all things in this fleeting world are impermanent and should be considered to be illusions. They are like a star at dawn, a bubble in a stream, a flash of lightning in a summer cloud, a flickering lamp, a phantom, or a dream. This is the meaning of the Diamond Cutter sutra."

The Abbot nodded to the circle of monks, and they began to chant. Some of the novices read the sutra from little books they carried in their jackets. Each time they reached the end they would begin again. When the incense sticks burned out one of the novices would replace them. They chanted for hours, non-stop. Xing Bo slid out of the circle and curled up on the wooden floor to nap. Jeff tried to keep his eyes open, but he kept drifting off, his head slowly drooping and then snapping back up as he caught himself. He tried to think of Jillian as "a flash of lightning in a summer cloud." The monks' voices turned to a drone that filled his head. Eventually the sound pushed out all of his thoughts. The floor no longer hurt his butt, the incense no longer stung his eyes, he was no longer embarrassed by Xing Bo's snoring.

At last someone rang the bell in the tower next to the prayer hall. The monks stopped chanting and stood up, stretching. Jeff remained seated, rubbing his eyes. As the monks filed out of the hall he shook Xing Bo.

"Wake up, man. It's over."

They walked back in the dark to the big room that served as a dormitory for the foreign students. Liu Tsu met them outside the door with a flurry of angry Chinese. Jeff turned to Xing Bo. "What's he saying?"

"Everyone's asleep. He's angry that we didn't tell him where we were, and he blames me. He says he will tell Master when he sees him in order to make trouble for me."

Jeff looked at Liu Tsu and held up his middle finger. "Ask him if he knows what this means."

Xing Bo laughed. "He knows."

Jeff woke the next morning to the sound of people arguing. He pulled on his pants and ambled outside where Xing Bo and the three Brits were sitting on the steps, eating breakfast and watching Shi De Jun yell at Liu Tsu. He looked a question at Xing Bo.

"Master refuses to fire me," he said. "Also, there will be no training today. You are all going stair running." He pointed to the pagoda on the mountain peak. "Up there."

It was just the five of them, Shi De Jun drove back down the mountain and Xing Bo stayed behind at the temple.

They slung bags filled with bottled water across their backs and started up. An ancient stone staircase wound its way through the forest to the top. Liu Tsu estimated that it would take them five hours going up and four hours coming down. Chris and Mark led the way, and Liu Tsu walked up behind the group, yelling at them when they stopped to rest. Jeff kept pace with Lon, mostly to have someone to talk to, but after the first hour they could barely breathe, let alone talk.

By the time they reached the top Jeff was drenched with sweat. His back ached where the water bottles had bounced against his spine, and he was shaking. The top of the mountain was sheathed in mist, and the cool air felt good. Next to the pagoda was the shrine, and next to the shrine was a woman in a blue windbreaker with a little food cart. Jeff was amazed to see anyone else at the top. He walked around behind the shrine and saw the woman's minivan and the dirt track that disappeared into the pines. He bought a ball of sticky rice wrapped in a banana leaf and a bean paste bun and flopped down next to Chris and Mark. They were sitting in the shade playing with a little white kitten. Lon collapsed next to them a few minutes later and, finally, Liu Tsu came strolling up. He sat down a little apart from the group and drank the Coke he had bought from the vending cart.

"Wicked run, eh, mates?" Mark said.

Lon lay back and closed his eyes.

"I didn't think I was going to make it," Jeff said. "I'm glad this food cart's here, or you'd have to carry me back down."

"Or," Lon said, his eyes still closed, "we could leave you for the vultures. That's for me, boys. Just write my Da, and tell him I'm bird food."

Liu Tsu came over to play with the kitten that was chewing on Chris' shoe. He pulled a thread off one of his socks and tied a twig to it. The kitten rolled on its back and started batting at the twig as Liu Tsu dangled it over him.

I guess the guy's human after all, Jeff thought. When Liu Tsu looked at him he smiled. "Cute kitten," he said.

Liu Tsu smiled back. He picked the kitten up, held it about eight inches off the ground and dropped it. The kitten landed on its side.

"What the hell's he doing with that cat?" Chris asked.

Liu Tsu extended his flat palm and made a flipping gesture.

"I think he's trying to see if it will land on its feet," Mark said.

"Well he better cut it out. The thing belongs to that woman with the cart."

Liu Tsu picked the kitten up again. He stood up and extended his arm. The kitten dropped from about five feet. It landed on its hind feet and chest. It yelped and started to run toward the food cart, but before it could get away Liu Tsu grabbed it. All three Brits were yelling at him now. He grinned and pretended to throw the kitten into the air.

"Hey, uncool, mate," Lon said. "Leave the cat alone."

Jeff pushed himself to his feet, walked over to Liu Tsu, and took the kitten out of his hands.

He turned toward the food cart, and Liu Tsu punched him in the back of the head. Jeff fell forward, catching himself before he hit the ground. He sat down, released the kitten and rocked back and forth, holding his head. Lon shouted, "Bloody hell!"

Liu Tsu grabbed the kitten and tossed him high over his head, into the air. The kitten landed on his back and lay there, gasping for air. Jeff let go of his head and got up. His face was red. He walked up to Liu Tsu.

"What the hell is wrong with you?" he shouted.

Liu Tsu hit him in the nose, breaking it instantly. The Brits were on their feet now, shouting at Liu Tsu, and the woman from the vending cart was cradling her kitten in her arms. Jeff wasn't aware of anything but Liu Tsu's foot, rising from the ground in an arc aimed at his head. He stepped into Liu Tsu, jamming the kick and sending him sprawling. Liu Tsu hopped up and came at him. He feinted a front kick but jabbed high, aiming for Jeff's nose again. Jeff was up on his toes. He danced back and to one side, and when Liu Tsu put his foot down from the kick, Jeff moved in and slammed a roundhouse kick into Liu Tsu's knee. The knee buckled and when he tried to stand on it, broke. Liu Tsu hit the ground screaming and holding his leg.

Jeff turned to Lon. "The cat," he shouted. "Where's the cat?" Lon brought the woman over to show Jeff the kitten in her arms. It was purring and batting at the strings of her windbreaker. Jeff walked into the woods, lay down under a pine tree, and cried. His anguished sobs filled the forest and poured down the mountainside.

The Brits carried Liu Tsu down the mountain. It took them five hours, and he screamed the whole way. The next day Shi De Jun drove Jeff to the train station in Zhengzhou. It was an hour's drive, and neither man said a word.

STIGMATA

Cathy opened the kitchen door to the smell of marijuana, and her palms began to itch. She didn't know if it was men that caused her mother to have low self-esteem or low self-esteem that caused her mother to hook up with one loser after another. Bob was the latest. As far as Cathy could determine, Bob's appeal lay primarily in his ability to keep her mother supplied with high quality pot. Cathy sighed and tossed her jacket and book bag on one of the empty chairs at the kitchen table. She scratched her palms through her purple knit gloves.

"You're late," her mother said. "Did you stay after school for something?"

"Today's Wednesday. I tutor grade school kids on Wednesdays."

"Right. How'd it go?"

"Fine. You promised you'd quit smoking pot, Mom. It's my birthday present. Remember?"

"Yes, and I also remember that your birthday's not until next week.

"You know it makes me worry about you." She pleaded. "Please."

Cathy took a can of soda from the refrigerator and sat down across the table from her mother. In addition to an overflowing ashtray and a toaster, the table was covered with cheese sandwiches. Cathy nodded toward the pile.

"Bad case of the munchies?"

Her mother held up a sheet of aluminum foil and a small utility knife. She grinned. "I'm making miracles." She handed Cathy a sandwich and went back to work, cutting small pieces from the sheet of foil. Cathy took a bite of the sandwich and grimaced. She washed it down with soda.

"This is awful."

"You're supposed to look at it, not eat it. Turn it over."

Cathy looked at the other side of the sandwich. A brown pattern, three shades darker than the rest of the toast, portrayed a familiar looking face. Above the face floated an oval shape.

"That's one of my earlier efforts. See, I wrap the bread in foil before I toast it. Where the foil's cut away, the bread gets darker. The difficult part was figuring out how long to toast it. Finally I decided to try a double thickness of foil. That did the trick. I get a cleaner line and a darker image." She fished a half-smoked joint from the ashtray, caught the look on Cathy's face, and put it back. "What do you think?"

"What do I think about what? I don't even know what I'm looking at. Who is this supposed to be?"

"Why, it's Saint Catherine of course."

Saint Catherine was the patron saint of Sienna, the Italian town that Cathy's grandparents had immigrated from. Cathy's father had named her for the saint, and when she was a little girl he had insisted she dress in jumpers covered with yellow lilies, the symbol of Saint Catherine. Cathy first read about Saint Catherine in *A Child's Book of Saints*. Cathy's father gave her the book on her seventh birthday. As a young girl Saint Catherine had exhibited the stigmata, and a dove floated continuously over her head. She was also able to fly up the stairs of her family's small Siennese home to her bedroom. Cathy thought how wonderful it would be to float up stairs like Saint Catherine, her feet dangling a few inches from the ground. She was glad not to have a dove floating over her head, though. She imagined Saint Catherine, covered in bird crap.

"Okay, I'll bite. Why are you putting Saint Catherine on a cheese sandwich?"

"To sell on eBay."

"You're high," Cathy said.

"That's got nothing to do with it. People buy religious icons on eBay all the time. Last year a potato chip shaped like the Holy Virgin sold for eleven thousand dollars."

"So, you think someone will buy a sandwich with a picture of Saint Catherine on it?"

"Not just a picture, a mystical image that magically appeared on it."

Cathy looked at the sandwich in her hand and tossed it on the table. "They don't even taste good. Anyway, put aside for a moment the fact that it's unethical and unsanitary, no one knows what Saint Catherine looked like. This could be anyone."

"Not just anyone," her mother said. She held up a photograph. Cathy looked close. The image on the mystical sandwiches was her eighth-grade graduation photo.

"You suck," she said, and trudged up the stairs to her room. She flopped down on the bed and peeled off her gloves. Taped to both of her palms were large cotton bandages, stained red. Cathy pulled off the tape and tossed the bandages on the floor. Blood lightly oozed from the unbroken skin of her palms.

o

Cathy was leaning on the counter, grading papers from the math class she tutored, when Grace shuffled into the Coffee Clutch, towing two big garbage bags and the odor of unwashed clothes and rotting food. A table of customers picked up their cups and moved to the back of the room.

"Hi Cathy," she shouted. "Happy birthday."

Cathy looked up and waved. "Hiya babe. Thanks for remembering." She set down her papers and moved toward the espresso machine. "The usual?"

"You bet," Grace said.

They had met on Cathy's first day of work. Grace had come in to con someone out of a free cup of coffee and Cathy made her a cappuccino. She told Grace that drinking cappuccino instead of coffee would show people that she had sophisticated tastes. Grace had told Cathy about the job she used to have, washing floors at the college. She liked that job, she said, but when her mother died she had moved into the halfway house and it was too far to commute. Cathy figured that, physically, Grace was close to forty. Mentally she was still a child.

Grace stood at the counter sipping her cappuccino and licking the foam off her lips. "You know who would like this?" Grace asked.

"Your mother?"

"You bet!"

Grace started every conversation with a reference to her mother. In fact, Grace told the same stories over and over but Cathy always listened. Making lattes for harried yuppies and demanding housewives had made her aware of how easy it is to have your dignity trod upon.

"So what's on the schedule for today, Grace?"

Grace smiled over the rim of her cup. "I've got a date."

"Hey, that's great! Who's your date with?"

"A guy I met on the internet. We have a computer at the house, and I met a guy in a chat room. His name is Dawg, and he's going to take me to the movies."

"Dog?"

"Well, it's really Doug, but he calls himself Dawg on the internet. He's very nice. We're going to the movies, and after we're going to a restaurant."

A line of customers was starting to form at the register. Cathy took a few drink orders and moved back to the espresso machine. She turned the valve to clear the steam wand and forgot to turn it off again before putting the wand in the milk pitcher. There was a hiss and a plume of hot milk shot up. She ignored it. "Have you ever met this guy?" she asked.

"No, but he says he wants to be my boyfriend. We're going to the Rialto."

"The Rialto? Grace, that's clear across town. Is he picking you up?"

"No. I'm going to take the bus and meet him there.

I've got to go home and get ready now. I just came in to tell you because you and me get along so well."

Cathy's palms felt damp under the rubber gloves she always wore at work. She hoped it was just perspiration. "Well now, Grace, let's think about this for a minute." She turned to hand out finished drinks to waiting customers and when she turned back Grace was already at the door.

"I gotta go get ready, Cathy. I'll come by tomorrow and tell you all about it."

o

"Look out, Kimberly, here comes The Bloody Paw."

"Ooooo. I'm so scared. Don't get blood on me, Bloody."

"That freak is a walking horror show. Get away from me, freak."

A week ago Mrs. Gordimer, the new gym teacher, had forced Cathy to take her gloves off in class. She had tried to explain that she had permission to wear them due to a medical condition, but Mrs. Gordimer wouldn't listen. Volleyball, she said, must be played barehanded. Within days the whole school knew about the spontaneous bleeding on Cathy's palms. Now she marched from class to class, head down, books clutched to her chest. She had never been popular, but now even the few friends she had no longer associated with her. The other kids smelled her fear and tore at her like a pack of hyenas.

"Fuck off, bitch," she muttered.

Kimberly stepped in front of her, blocking her path. "What did you say to me, Bloody Paw?"

Cathy stopped. She stared at Kimberly's shoes. "Move please."

"I want to know what you called me," said Kimberly.

Cathy tensed. Two weeks, she decided, was long enough. She was through being bullied. She looked Kimberly in the face.

"Move please," she repeated.

Kimberly turned to the crowd that was forming and shrugged her shoulders in mock bewilderment.

"See," she said, "this is what we have to put up with. This infected bitch, just walking around the halls, being all nasty and shit."

Cathy set her books on the floor. Then she pulled the purple knit glove from her right hand and smacked Kimberly in the face with an open palm. Kimberly stumbled backward, a shiny wet smear across her nose and forehead. She scrubbed her face with the sleeve of her blouse and screamed when it came away red.

"Oh my God!"

Cathy turned to face the group of kids that had gathered behind her. She raised her hand over her head.

"Who's next?" she shouted. "Who wants to be infected?"

o

Two years after Cathy's parents were divorced her father's liver gave out. His new wife didn't have the money or inclination to bury him so, finally, Cathy's mother agreed to do it. Cathy barely recognized the disease-shrunken man in the casket, but she sat with him in the funeral home all day. When Bob made a joke about not being able to cremate him because of his dangerously high alcohol content Cathy told him to keep his shitty remarks to himself. Right before they closed the casket she laid a yellow lily on her father's chest.

She had vowed not to think about him after he left but in fact, she thought about him all the time. She thought about all his fatherly endearments like, "How's my little saint this morning?" and "Heal any lepers at school today, honey?" It was because of her father that she tutored underprivileged children after school and volunteered at a soup kitchen on the weekends. It was because of him that she had never been on a date. She had been asked out a couple of times, but she had always been too busy. If he wanted his daughter to be a saint, she would be.

Sitting in front of his casket she remembered how, when she was a little girl, he would let her sit on his lap and steer their old Volkswagen, even in the snow, and how he smelled like cinnamon gum and how he was always singing old Beatles songs. Mostly though, she remembered worrying about him. Her mother had left him because he couldn't control his alcoholism. He had always had a drinking problem, but after the divorce it had grown worse. He hadn't called her in two months, and she hadn't seen him in six.

She didn't want to worry about him, it made her palms bleed, but she couldn't help it. "Maybe now," she thought, "it will stop. Please, God, make it stop."

o

The Coffee Clutch was empty and Cathy was worried. It had been over a month since she'd last seen Grace and she imagined her corpse lying face down in some alley. She wished she knew the address of the halfway house where Grace lived. She had gotten a list of nearby halfway houses from the county health department. None of them had a resident named Grace.

Cathy stared out the window, watching the evening commuters dart from awning to doorway as they tried to avoid the constant drizzle. She saw Grace cross the street, being led by her reflection on the damp pavement.

"Hi Cathy."

"Hiya babe, long time, no see. Where've you been?"

Grace looked down at her feet. "Oh, I don't know."

"Last time we talked you had a date. How'd it go?"

Grace spoke without looking up. "He didn't show up. I waited for him for five hours, and then the busses stopped running, so I had to call Mrs. Barnes at the house to come and get me. She was pretty mad. I talked to him in the chat room the next day. He called me an idiot. He kept typing LOL."

Cathy's eyes filled with tears. "Oh Grace," she said. "I'm so sorry."

"That's okay," Grace said. "When I was in school people called me names all the time. My mother used to tell me not to let them needle me."

Cathy came out from behind the counter and hugged her. She felt a trickle of blood run down her wrist.

○

Cathy slept in until almost noon. She pulled her robe on and shuffled out to the kitchen in search of coffee. There was a note from her mother on the kitchen table.

Sweetie. Bob and I are going to a concert over in Lynchburg. We won't be back until late. I made a casserole for you. It's in the fridge next to the cheesecake. Enjoy your Saturday. Love you, Mom

Cathy was scheduled to work at the soup kitchen at 2:00. Instead she decided to go to the cemetery.

The bus dropped her off just down the block from the cemetery gate, and she hiked in, cutting across the rolling hills of dead, winding her way between the stones. She could never find the grave but had learned to look for Kaminski, Stuart and Evelyn. They had a marble cherub with a missing wing on their stone. From there it was a beeline up a small hill to her father's grave. A light drizzle was falling but she had brought a heavy coat. Besides, it was quiet and the slick, newly cut grass smelled fresh and alluring. The lilies were gone from her father's vase so she unwrapped the new ones she had brought, dropped them in and sat.

"This has got to stop," she said. She looked down at the grave. "It's messed up my whole life. I don't want to worry about other people all the time. I can't even read a newspaper because it gets soaked with blood. I want to go to concerts and have a boyfriend. I want to be normal." She lay down on her father's grave. Wet grass clippings clung to her cheek. "I don't want to do this anymore," she said. "I quit."

The drizzle was stronger now, not quite rain, but enough to soak her hair. A trickle ran down her face, and when she wiped it she realized she was crying. She sat up, peeled her gloves off, and looked at her palms. Rivulets of blood mixed with the rain. "Oh, hell," she said.

With an effort, she pushed herself to her feet. Looking down, past the wrought iron fence, she could see the bus coming, still a few blocks away. She pulled on her gloves and started back down the hill.

THE METAL TEETH OF THE MONSTER

Sunday mornings is when we race the freights. Frank and Gerald and I are supposed to be in Sunday school, but we ditch a couple of times a month and walk downtown. Sometimes we go to the Walgreen's to look at magazines, but then we go down to the tracks and wait. The freights slow to a walk when they come into town. When they get to York Street they start to speed up again. That's where we start running. We run on the track bed, right next to the trains.

○

I'm running fast. I'm running so fast that my suit coat is flapping against my back. I take off my tie and stuff it into my pocket. It's too tight anyway. I stay right next to the train for awhile, and then I start to cut loose. I love to pass the cars—flatbeds, tankers, boxcars. I run past an open boxcar. It's going so slow that I could grab the ladder and swing myself up and ride it to Iowa or California or wherever it's going. For a second I imagine my mom, sitting alone at the dinner table, wondering where I am. Wondering if I'm dead or alive. Wondering if I'm at my dad's place in Santa Rosa. She has a plate of potatoes and corn, but she isn't eating. She just pushes it around with her fork and stares at the empty chair across the table.

I time my strides to the clacking of the huge wheels. The sun flashes off one as it turns. It looks like one of those knives people use to slice pizza. It'd slice you up good if you fell under it. I saw a movie once where a guy fell, and a train cut his leg off. You've got to be careful. I don't want to look around, but I do. Frank is right behind me, running hard, and Gerald, that stupid fuck, is wheezing along behind him. Gerald's face is red.

o

I met Frank and Gerald in Sunday school about a year ago. At first, I thought Gerald was shy because he didn't talk much, even when it was just the three of us. Then he started to say things. Every time I'd tell a joke he'd say, "Heard it!" right before the punch line. Or if I'd mention that I liked some girl he'd grab his dick and make kissing noises. I wouldn't care but Frank always laughs at his stupid cracks.

Sometimes Gerald doesn't want to race the freights so we walk back to the church and hang out in the parking lot until the service lets out. He says he's worried that his parents are going to find out we've been ditching, but I think he's afraid of the trains.

The way we got started racing trains, we were talking about Heaven and Hell and the other stuff we had learned in Sunday school. I said if Heaven was so great why didn't we all just live there to begin with? Why even fool around with the earth? God could take us all up there whenever He wanted to, couldn't He?

I came up with the idea of racing the trains. I used to

be afraid of them when I was a little kid. One time, Mom and I were sitting at a railroad crossing, waiting for the train to pass. Ours was the first car in line, and I must have looked nervous or something because she looked at me and said, "Watch out! The monster is going to get you." Then she laughed.

Some day Frank and I are going to run ahead and jump across the tracks in front of the train. We haven't done it yet, though. We always chicken out at the last second.

o

I run next to the space between the cars, so I can look at the coupling. It looks like two right hands, gripping each other's fingers. The brake cable is swinging below it. The town flashes by through the gap. The Walgreen's, the pizza place, the Dairy Queen and then, when I can see the dry cleaners, the train speeds up. I turn and shout, "Let's go!" to Frank, and then I start to pour it on. Even with my church shoes on I can feel my toes grab the earth. The gravel crunches under my feet, and the dust feels sharp and hot in my nose. I'm so fast that grasshoppers are leaping to get out of my way, popping up just as I get to them. A sea of grasshoppers parts ahead of me. I hear Frank shout, "Come on Gerald, come on."

o

Frank lives across town, so on Saturday we ride our bikes and meet up somewhere, the mall or maybe down by the creek. Sometimes we throw a ball around, but usually we just talk. One Saturday we took some cheese and beef jerky and Cokes out to Grauie Mill. It's this place where they have an old fashioned grinding stone for making flour that's powered by a water wheel in the creek. We waded across the dam next to the wheel and sat on this little island while we ate. I told

Frank about the time I rode my bike back and forth in front of Gretchen Kirstner's house for an hour, hoping she'd come outside but also afraid she'd see me riding back and forth. He told me about the time his dad slapped his mom around, so he and his mom stayed at a motel for a few nights. I told Frank that I think Gerald is an idiot, and Frank said that he and Gerald have been friends since the third grade and I should shut up about him.

o

The engineer sees me as I pull even with him, and he waves me away. I just grin. He shouts something, but the chugging of the engine and the sound of my blood pumping in my ears drowns him out. My heart sounds like it's going to pop, but I don't care; I feel great. The train is going faster now. I lean into it, and my thighs and calves are like iron bars, cutting through the air, pushing me forward. I'm up on my toes. My feet touch the ground just long enough. I'm out in front by three feet, then five feet, then ten feet, then I cut left. I jump and time slows, and as I sail across the tracks I look at the horrible metal teeth of the monster. When my feet hit I throw myself forward and roll down the bank, into the weeds. As I get up I can see, flickering on and off between the cars, Frank and Gerald, standing on the other side.

FEAR

You and Nancy roar, sticky in the night, with the windows down and the 8-track kicking out *Evil Ways* and *Jingo*, and the miracle of evaporation draws the sweat and alcohol from your skins. She turns off the music when she sees the fires. Six, no eight maybe, and you drive down the hill toward them, slowly. There are figures moving, running in and out of the flames. You turn at the dirt track that leads to the first in a row of blazing shacks. The sky is empty except for a moon that traces the edges of the smoke with silver. The firelight makes the shadows quiver. It's beautiful until someone screams. Then the smoke hurts your eyes, and you hear crying.

A voice at the car window asks, "What you doin' here?" The flames reveal a man with walnut colored skin. You say, "We saw the fire from the road. Can we help?"

He looks at Nancy. Her eyes are enormous.

"You'd best be goin'. The Klan's burning people out. There'll be trouble."

You drive. Nancy cries.

"Don't be afraid," you say.

"I'm not," she says. "I'm sad."

o

"Let's dance," she says, in her whiskeyed, Marilyn Monroe voice. The words waver, slowly, like the Spanish moss hanging from the trees outside the bar. As soon as she says it the music stops. A room full of afternoon drunks turns to look at the whirling blonde at your side. Bleary eyes note your shoulder-length hair and scruffy teen-age beard. An enormous pyramid of empty beer cans leers down at you from the center table. Nancy sways too close, and a drunken Alabamian syrups, "The hell!" You grab a handful of Nancy and spin her toward the door.

Sitting in the car she says, "We're Yankees. We're stoned. We should go."

You drive, Nancy laughs, excited by her fear.

"I love you," you say.

"Thanks," she says.

o

You watch the road with one eye and Nancy, curled sideways, dozing, with the other. She makes you afraid. Not afraid of rednecks, afraid of kissing, of not kissing, of fumbling. Your first time was in the basement of the Methodist church with a girl you never saw again. You didn't think about blaspheming. You were listening to your hormones. You see Nancy's dandelion hair and pale fingernails. She's your church now, but you see the indifference in her walk, always a little ahead of, not with. You see it in her dance. She will dance with you or with someone else or alone.

o

The sand is white, the water is blue, and the car is

parked under a long empty bridge. You walk in the warm surf and watch the gulls, and when you look back the car is tiny. Nancy naps on the back seat. You stop and stare out at the flat blue horizon. The receding water sucks the sand from under your feet, and you sink a little. You wonder who Nancy will, someday, decide to love.

THE END OF SUMMER

Bethea thought that the August air smelled like an opera, thick and interminable. She was trying on the shoes she found in her grandmother's wardrobe, balancing on one leg while looking in the mirror, when her perspiration damp skin snagged the hem of her skirt, and she fell. From her new position on the floor the room looked old and dirty. The house was an old lady's museum, filled with figurines and collectibles. When she and her brother were children they got a whupping whenever they came to visit. Their play had always ended with damage to some knickknack. Grandmother kept a switch by the kitchen door.

Her grandmother had been dead for over a month, but her mother still wasn't coping. The old woman had been stern, as unyielding as an iron bar, and she had bound Momma to her with her will. Now that she was dead Momma was lost, and it fell to Bethea to sort through the mountain of her possessions. School was going to start in less than three weeks, and she hadn't bought her books. She desperately wanted to go to Julliard. She had applied but had never heard from them. Every day, for months, she came straight home from school to check the mail. Nothing. Momma begged her to go to the community college. They were a family of three, after all, and Momma couldn't handle James alone. The community college had a small music department; it would have to do.

She lay on the carpet wishing she had been accepted at Julliard. It offered her sanctuary from the responsibilities of her emotional dependents, a brother disabled at birth and a mother disabled by life. She looked under the wardrobe. Something sparkled.

o

James always carried fifty cents in his front pocket. Bethea gave him the money every morning, and she always said, "Put it in your front pocket so you don't lose it." Fifty cents was enough for a jawbreaker at the Speedimart.

His hand was already sticky with a mixture of orange juice and dirt when he jammed it into his pocket to dig for the coins. The man behind the counter glared as he fished out one filthy object after another.

Two lug nuts.

Customers were starting to line up behind him.

A plastic army man.

Mrs. Bensen was getting milk from the cooler.

A crumpled white envelope.

The man behind him coughed.

Fifty cents.

He wiped the sweat from his forehead with the back of his grimy hand and turned his attention to the candy. The cellophane slid neatly off and fluttered to the floor. The jawbreaker popped into his mouth as he opened the door. He was almost outside when the clerk shouted, "Hey, dummy. Pick up that wrapper."

o

Bethea was sitting on the floor in the middle of the living room, surrounded by an army of porcelain figurines and blown glass animals. She was looking at her grandmother's earring and crying softly. She hadn't even liked the old woman, dammit. The earring was just junk, but there was something about the way it refracted the late afternoon sun that reminded her of all the time she'd spent as a little girl, sitting at her grandmother's vanity trying on jewelry and listening to old records. She was blowing her nose when the front door flew open and slammed against the wall. There was James, and he was crying too.

James was almost twenty and spent most of his time watching cartoons on television. He was older than her by two years, but his intellectual development had stopped when he was about seven. Now he was standing there, crying and trying to talk at the same time. The jawbreaker in his mouth muffled his speech.

"Slow down," she said. "I can't understand what you're saying."

James opened his hand and spit the jawbreaker out. It bounced off his palm and arced through the air, a glistening blue meteor. It took out the most elaborate figurine first. The young man kneeling before the pretty girl on the park bench was decapitated. A cherub lost its wings. The jawbreaker clacked on the tabletop and went spinning off to rest among the shards of a former herd of glass horses.

James eyed the destruction with open-mouthed

curiosity. He poked a little bird with his index finger and jumped when its beak broke off.

"Oh, man," he said, "Now I'm gonna get it."

Bethea laughed.

"What's funny?" he asked.

"Nothing. That was cool. What were you trying to say?"

"The man at the store called me a dummy again."

"Now, what did we agree on the last time that happened?"

James grinned. "That he don't know me, so screw him."

"That's right, he doesn't know you. If he knew you like I do, he'd know that you're not a dummy." She patted the carpet. "Sit down here and talk for awhile."

James dug the envelope out of his pocket and plopped down, cross-legged, in front of Bethea.

"What's that?" she asked.

"I been saving this for you. Momma threw it in the trash, but I knew you wanted it." He held it out. Bethea took the envelope. It was from Julliard.

The last rays of the fading summer sun had turned the room orange. James picked up the little severed head and set it on the pretty girl's lap.

WHAT STAYS

One night, as I was making love to the woman who would become my wife, I suddenly stopped moving. Her eyelids were half closed, and her mouth was half open, and her breathing, quick and throaty, was the only sound in the room.

"Be still," I said. "I want to stay inside you and burn the image of your face into my retinas so that, no matter what I look at from now on, you will be superimposed on top of it."

Her eyes got big and wet, and she bit my shoulder and pulled me into her, trying to fuse us together on the tiny bed in her tiny dorm room. A contraband black kitten slept on her grandmother's green-starred quilt. I smelled like cigarettes; she smelled like almond soap. I remember what I said and did and saw and heard and smelled and tasted that night. My thumb even remembers the soft fluff of her eyebrow as it traced the arc above her eye. I remember what I thought, but I've forgotten how it felt. I guess I was happy, but for some reason the memory of that happiness didn't stay with me. I mean, I can associate that night with the word happiness, but a word is just a symbol; it's not happiness, not really.

Then we were married, and a lot of other things happened. It doesn't matter what. They've probably happened to you or to someone you know. You don't need me to tell you about having jobs and children and going shopping and looking for a parking spot that's a little closer to the store and watching the replication of joyous events slowly erode their meaning. Only so many birthdays, holidays and family vacations can be special.

One night, after the affair and before the divorce, I was lying in the dark next to my wife, amazed that the bed could feel so empty with both of us in it. I said, "Don't you think there's some way to fix this?"

She may have replied or not. I don't recall.

I said, "Don't you want to fix this?"

She turned away from me, on to her side. I crossed the chasm and put my arm around her. She pulled away.

"Don't touch me," she said.

Then there was pain everywhere. My head throbbed. My chest was filled with sharp things. I couldn't breathe.

Now, there's a feeling I can remember.

CRIMINALITY

THE SEED

The man grumbled as he shoved the gate open against the weight of the new snow, pushing the drift up against the garage and clearing a path through to the yard. A few flakes, dislodged from the eaves, settled on the shoulders of his shiny, black leather coat. A little brown and white terrier lay on a lawn chair under the protection of a large awning. As the man approached, the afternoon sun stretched his shadow across the snow, alerting the dog who ran to the end of his chain and yapped at him. He showed the dog the short length of two-by-four in his hand. "Shut up, rat," he said.

Opening the screen door he pulled a small screw jack from his pocket and held it against the doorframe, opposite the lock. Then he wedged the two-by-four between the jack and the other side of the frame. Four, quick turns of the jack bowed the doorframe out in the center, just enough to slip the lock. He pushed the door open, knocked the jack and two-by-four out of the way and started to enter. As an afterthought he kicked the snow off his boots and wiped them on the mat.

Inside, the baby-blue kitchen walls were covered with

plaques that offered cute sayings like, *Bless This Mess* and *Kiss The Cook*. Toaster, blender and mixer were lined up, gleaming, on the counter. Everything was clean and tidy. The messiest thing in the room was the refrigerator. It was covered with dozens of photographs—pictures of family events. Smiling faces looked out from birthday parties, picnics, and graduation ceremonies. The people in the pictures seemed to be staring out at him, judging him. *Screw 'em*, he thought. He pulled a pair of latex gloves on, took out a can of spray paint and went to work, covering each smiling face with a patch of red, blotting out the mocking smiles. He stepped back to view the results, shook the can, and walked down the hallway to the living room.

o

Sean McKinney didn't like waking in a strange bed, not even the foldout couch in his mother's condo. He was disoriented and not quite sure where he was, in space or time. He briefly looked for Catherine on the other side of the bed, and then he remembered—cancer, the hospital, the funeral. It had been over a year, but he wasn't used to it. *You don't get used to losing your wife*, he thought, *you just become functional*.

The sound of clinking silverware woke him the rest of the way, and he heard the rumble of voices from the kitchen, his mother and his daughter. By the time he had dressed and folded up the sofa bed they had coffee poured and eggs on plates. He made his way through the piles of opened boxes and crumpled wrapping paper, past the artificial Christmas tree, and slid into his seat at the kitchen table. He began spooning sugar into his coffee.

"Deluxe service," he said. "What did I do to deserve this?"

His mother stood over him, kissed him on the top of the head, and brushed his sandy hair back from his eyes. She was a small woman, with dyed red hair that failed to disguise her age. "Not what you did, sweetie. What you're going to do."

His daughter chimed in. "Yeah, Dad. It'll be fun."

"What?" he asked. "What'll be fun?"

His mother smiled and handed him a plate of raisin toast. "Angelina and I want to go to the Raptor Center today."

"And be eaten by dinosaurs? No thanks."

"It's U of M's rehabilitation center for birds of prey," she said.

"Rehab center, eh. What are they addicted to, chihuahuas?"

"C'mon, Dad." Angelina winked at her grandmother. "It's ed-u-cational," she said.

McKinney started to object but his mother gave him The Look. The look that said, *you're doing this buster so just shut up and get with the program.* She was famous for The Look. It had worked on him when he was a child, and it had worked on his father.

Standing next to a cage containing a one-legged hawk, McKinney and his mother talked while Angelina moved from cage to cage, taking pictures of injured owls and fledgling eagles. McKinney watched his sixteen-year-old daughter and sighed. "She still cries herself to sleep, sometimes."

"It's hard to lose someone you love that much," his

mother said. "I know. And they were so close. Time will surely help."

"You're right, Mom. This trip is good for her. She likes coming to visit you."

McKinney's mother put her hand on his arm. "And how are you holding up, honey?"

"Better, I guess. I still think about Catherine all the time, but it doesn't immobilize me the way it used to."

"You know," she said, "since Angelina taught me to use a computer we've been corresponding by email. She says that sometimes you just sit, staring, for hours. And sometimes you forget to shave, and you go to work looking rumpled."

"I'll be all right."

She gave his arm a little squeeze. "I know you will, dear. It's Angelina I'm worried about. She needs her father to be strong for her."

"I... You're right, of course." He looked down at his feet. "She probably doesn't feel very secure, taken care of. Truth is, she's usually the one who gets dinner together. I don't seem to have much of an appetite these days."

"Look after your child, honey." She paused. "And how are things at the crime lab?"

"Okay. I was afraid they were going to fire me for a while. I fell way behind in my casework, had a big backlog. A couple of my cases got nollied."

"Nollied?"

"Nolle prosequi. It's Latin. Means the State's Attorney had to drop the case. It's one of the cardinal sins of the justice system. I'm all caught up now, though."

"Well, that's good because I have a favor to ask you."

"I'm on vacation, Mom."

"I know, but this won't take you very long. I have a friend whose husband was killed by a hit and run driver. The police have a suspect, and they've impounded his car, but the detective doesn't think he has enough evidence to charge him. I promised my friend that my son, the forensic scientist, would read the detective's report and let him know if anything looked odd."

"How did she get hold of the report?"

"She was the detective's Sunday school teacher when he was a little boy. They're still close."

Angelina bounced over from a nearby window. "What're we talking about, guys?"

"Your grandmother is trying to get me to work on my vacation."

"And your father is trying to get out of it."

Angelina hugged her grandmother. "You won, right?" she asked.

McKinney's mother gave him The Look. Angelina punched her father on his shoulder. "Ha," she said. "Girl power!"

o

That evening after dinner McKinney's mother handed him a folder containing reports related to the case of Thomas Jacobs, the man killed by the hit and run driver. McKinney plopped down on the couch, next to the Christmas tree. Red and green lights colored the pages in the folder as he pored through them. Angelina went across the street to visit a girl she had met during her last visit.

The first report in the folder was from the Medical

Examiner's office. It detailed the autopsy, listing the man's injuries and described the samples that had been taken to send to the toxicology lab. Jacobs' injuries had been extensive— broken ribs piercing his lungs, brain hemorrhage caused by blunt force trauma, massive blood loss, shattered pelvis, spinal cord damage. McKinney thought the man had probably died before the ambulance arrived. The last page contained the toxicology screen. There was no evidence of alcohol or drugs in the victim's system.

McKinney turned to the detective's report. Color copies of some of the crime scene photos were clipped to the front page. He leafed through them. Jacobs' body wasn't in any of the photos. The blood on the pavement was the only indication of where he had lain. Another photo showed a close up of broken bits of metal and plastic lying next to the curb. The crime scene investigators, no doubt, thought these could be pieces of the car that had broken off at impact. One of the photos showed an irregularly shaped piece of thick, black plastic. The ruler the photographer had placed next to it for scale indicated that it was about five inches by three inches. One of the short ends was smoothly curved, but the other end showed a jagged break. The material was covered with striations, no doubt part of the manufacturing process. If this piece had broken off the impounded car it would be easy to get a match and put the car at the crime scene. He flipped through the rest of the photos until he found the shots of the car. The bumper and the hood were both crumpled on the passenger side of the car, and the windshield had cracks that radiated out from an impact point. One photo showed a close up of the bumper. It was light blue, just like the car's body. Finally, he set the folder to one side, and sat staring off into space. He had seen the results of violence before, in person and in photographs. It was always unsettling. He wished Angelina would get home from visiting her friend. He set the folder down and went out to the kitchen.

"So, what do you think?" his mother asked.

"I don't know, Mom. I can't seem to focus. Thinking about death just makes me sad. This is the same thing that happens to me all the time at work. I see the results of senseless violence and start to shut down. I guess Catherine's death has made me kind of morose."

"Yes, but you'll survive it, Sean. Even when horrible things happen the world is still filled with beauty. Sunshine still filters through autumn leaves. Birds still soar and loop through the sky. And you have the honor of seeing one of nature's most beautiful shows, a child growing into young adulthood. You just need to start looking again."

McKinney walked to the balcony doors and peered out at the snow, watching it swirl up the side of the building. Being on the third floor gave him a nearly unobstructed view of the block. He could see Angelina's friend's house across the street. He could also see Angelina. She and another girl were running through the snow. They didn't run like children playing, they ran with a sense of urgency. They crossed the street, passed under a streetlight, and ran up the circular drive to the entrance of the condo building. *Something's up*, he thought.

o

The two girls stood in the middle of the living room in their coats and gloves, crying and dripping snow on the carpet. They were both trying to talk at the same time and McKinney couldn't understand a word they said. His mother heard the noise and came in from the kitchen. "Angelina, Jill, slow down, one at a time," she said.

The girls looked at one another. Jill sat on the carpet and started taking off her boots. Angelina began. "Someone broke into Jill's house and vandalized it. They spray painted all the walls and cut up the furniture."

Jill stopped pulling off her boots and started sobbing. McKinney's mother got down on the floor and put the girl's head on her shoulder. "Is your mother home, dear," she asked.

Jill was crying too hard to answer. "No, she's at work," Angelina said.

"Till ten," Jill added. She snuffled and wiped her nose with the back of her hand. "She cocktails over at the Ramada."

Swell, McKinney thought, a cocktail waitress. She's probably got dozens of stalkers. "Did you girls call the police?" he asked.

"I thought we should tell you, first, Dad," Angelina said. "So you can look for evidence before the police get here."

"That's not the way it works, Bella," he said. When Angelina was born McKinney had looked at the beautiful, brown-eyed baby nestled in his wife's arms and said, "Ciao, Bella." She had been Bella to him ever since. "The police are perfectly capable of finding evidence." He turned to Jill. "When did this happen?"

"I don't know," she said. "I spent all day with my

friends at the mall. When I came home to feed Big Bob I saw the back door was open."

McKinney interrupted. "Who's Big Bob?"

"That's their dog," Angelina said. "He's really cute."

"Anyway, I knew my mom had already gone to work, but I didn't know why the door was open, so I went in and everything was trashed." She started crying again. "I didn't know if I should call the police or something, so I've just been sitting on the floor in the living room, trying to figure what to do."

"We didn't touch anything, Dad," Angelina said.

"Except I used the bathroom," Jill said. "Angelina was the calm one. I was totally freaking out, but she said we should come and tell you."

McKinney tried to suppress a smile. "Good job, ladies." He picked up the telephone from a table in the entryway. "Let's call the police."

McKinney went downstairs to meet the two, uniformed officers. His mother stayed inside and called Jill's mother to tell her what had happened. She assured her that McKinney would take care of the house and that Jill was welcome to spend the night. The officers called it in, and evidence techs arrived a short while later. McKinney stayed outside when they went in the house to take photographs and look for fingerprints. They lifted a few prints off the doorframe and took samples of the red spray paint that defaced every room in the house. They bagged several empty paint cans and the screw jack and two-by-four that still lay by the back door. As they left they gave McKinney permission to clean up. He went in through the back door to look around. A little terrier click-clacked across the kitchen floor and stood looking up at him.

"You must be Big Bob," McKinney said. He picked up the dog. "You'd just be a snack to the dog I've got at home. Don't worry; he's vacationing at the kennel." He tucked Big Bob under his arm and carried him along as he walked from room to room, surveying the wreckage. Photographs coated with red paint had been strewn throughout the house. They mingled with fabric and stuffing from destroyed chairs and glass from broken lamps. Kitchen, master bedroom, bathroom, all had walls that had been defaced with red paint. In the living room the television lay on its back, its screen cracked and dented. The wall where it had stood now displayed the word, BITCH in drippy, three-foot high letters. A table-top Christmas tree had been thrown in the corner.

The only room not vandalized was Jill's bedroom. A herd of stuffed animals stared back at McKinney from the girl's pink bedspread. He looked at the dog. "Now, why do you suppose the vandals didn't trash this room?" Big Bob licked his face.

o

They decided to put the girls on the foldout couch in the spare room. McKinney, his gangly frame too tall for the sofa, curled up in a sleeping bag on the living room floor. He picked up the Thomas Jacobs case folder and flipped quickly past the photographs to the detective's report. His investigation had turned up no witnesses. McKinney could find no indication that the detective had submitted any evidence other than the plastic and metal found at the scene to the crime lab. McKinney rifled through the folder. There was no report from the crime lab. If this folder was complete it meant that the lab hadn't looked at any of the evidence. He tossed the folder aside and lay back, closing his eyes, pushing gift boxes of scarves and sweaters aside so he could stretch out. What, if anything, stood out from the reports? There was no lab report. Analyzing the bits found at the scene would be useless unless the detective had submitted a piece of the car itself for comparison. Wasn't there some part of the bumper or hood that should be examined? Were there paint chips at the scene that could be compared to the paint on the car?

He was awakened by the sound of a car door. The clock over the sofa read 2 a.m. He crawled out of the sleeping bag and went to the balcony doors to look out onto the street. The moon was up and the streetlights were still on, lighting up the block and the surrounding streets. A small, black sports car was parked in front of Jill's house and a woman in a white, down jacket and a Santa Claus cap was just getting out on the passenger side. She wore calf-high boots with furry trim around the top and carried a pair of pumps in one hand. She went to the back door first, saw where McKinney had boarded it up, and walked back out to the sidewalk to enter by the front door. She waggled her fingers at the driver of the sports car as she went inside. A red pickup truck drove past and turned at the corner. From McKinney's vantage point he saw the pickup pull into a driveway, back out into the street, and come around, passing the house again. A light came on in the living room, and McKinney saw the woman's silhouette cross the room. A few minutes later she came back out carrying a small suitcase. The sports car's trunk popped open and the woman tossed her bag in. She climbed into the passenger seat and the car whizzed off down the street.

The next morning McKinney sat talking with his mother over coffee. Angelina and Jill, having stayed awake most of the night, were still asleep. Big Bob was eating some chunks of liver sausage McKinney's mother had put down for him. McKinney stirred a couple of ice cubes into his coffee to bring its temperature down to a non-scalding level. "Call your friend," he said, "and tell her to call the detective and ask him to check under the crumpled section of the car's front bumper. When a car's bumper is the same color as the rest of the car it's usually just a plastic shell, put on the car for appearance. If they peel that shell off they'll find the real bumper underneath, and I'm willing to bet the real bumper is made of thick, black plastic similar to a piece of debris that was found at the crime scene. Tell her to have the detective pull the black bumper off the car and send it to the crime lab for comparison to that piece of plastic.

His mother grabbed a pencil and scribbled down the instructions. "Thank you, dear," she said. She turned from the counter and sat across the kitchen table from him. "Now, what are we going to do about this break-in?"

"I don't think there's much we can do beyond offering to take care of Jill. Her mother needs to talk to the police. She needs to go down to the station and file a complaint."

"Against who? The girls didn't see who did this and you know as well as I do that it wasn't a prank. Jill's mother is divorced, and they live in that house alone. The next time one of them could be at home when this maniac breaks in."

McKinney sighed. "Well, what do you think I can do? What would you like me to do?"

His mother sprinkled sugar over a grapefruit half and passed the bowl to McKinney. "I think you should catch the guy before he hurts someone."

"Catch him? I'm not a detective. I look at the evidence after a crime has been committed—in Illinois. Minneapolis has its own crime lab."

"Well, I think we need to question Jill's mother and find out if she suspects someone."

"And I think you watch too much TV."

"Yes, well, I've invited her for breakfast. Unless you want to meet her in your robe I suggest you change. And comb your hair, she'll be here any minute."

By the time McKinney got out of the bathroom Jill's mother was seated at the breakfast table, sipping coffee and taking tiny bites out of a sweet roll.

"Sean, this is Roberta Duncan."

The woman held out her hand. " Call me Bobbie," she said.

She was a short woman with a trim figure and mousey-brown hair pulled back from a large forehead. She wore a white running jacket with matching pants. McKinney caught a whiff of lavender mingled with tobacco smoke, and when he took her hand he noticed the nicotine stain on her thumb. She wore rings on all of her fingers.

They talked around the events of the previous night for a while, McKinney's mother saying what a nice girl Jill is, and Bobbie complimenting her on the condo's décor. Finally McKinney jumped in. "So, Bobbie, do you have any idea who vandalized your home? Who would want to terrorize you?"

She shook her head. "No, honestly, it makes no sense

to me."

"Problems at work?" he asked. "What about customers? Anyone giving you a hard time? Any stalkers?"

"No, it's a pretty quiet place. I don't date customers, but that hasn't been an issue for a while. I'm close to Lou, one of the bartenders, but it sure as shoot wasn't him, and the other two bartenders are women."

"Why are you certain it wasn't Lou?"

"We worked the same shift last night. He brought me home."

"Any problems with Jill? School trouble? Boyfriend trouble?"

She glared at McKinney over the top of her cup. "My daughter did not deface our home."

"Okay," McKinney said. "I'm just trying to cover all the bases. Her room was the only one not damaged. There must be some reason for that." He tried a different approach. "Do you know anyone who drives a red pickup truck?"

"Oh, god dammit." She slammed her coffee cup down, splashing liquid onto the table. "He's supposed to be in Oregon."

McKinney's mother reached over and blotted the spill with her napkin. "Who, dear?" she asked. "Who's supposed to be in Oregon?"

" Frank, my ex. After the divorce he went to stay at his momma and daddy's place near Eugene. The last I heard he had a job at a hardware store. He used to work construction. He's had one red pickup after another since I first met him. It's one of his things."

"His things?" McKinney asked.

"Yeah." Bobbie gave a quick, harsh laugh. "Frank thinks he's some kind of macho, cowboy character. He wears a leather coat and boots when he goes out, no matter if it's too hot. If he doesn't have his coat on he rolls his cigarette pack into the sleeve of his t-shirt. His pickup has a gun rack in the back window. Oh, and here's the kicker. He has a Marine Corps tattoo on his bicep, only Frank's never been in the military. Semper Fi my ass."

"When did you talk to him last?"

"Two weeks ago. I'm suing him for back child support. He called to tell me he got a letter from my lawyer and that I could go to hell."

McKinney's mother refilled Bobbie's coffee cup. "What about Jill?" she asked. "Doesn't he care about her feelings?"

"Oh, he's pissed at her, too. When he was leaving for Oregon he asked her if she wanted to go with him for a couple of months, visit her grandparents. She said no. Frank and Jill haven't gotten along since she became a teenager. It's a shame, they were real close when she was little." She took a sip of the fresh coffee. "He's kind of a control freak, which is why I gave him his walking papers."

After some coaxing from McKinney's mother, Bobbie agreed to let Jill spend a few days at the condo. "I'll take Big Bob home with me, though," she said. "You all don't need to be cleaning up dog poop." She also agreed to go to the police station and file a complaint against her ex-husband. McKinney hoped that, if he was still in the area, the police would pick him up quickly.

o

After Bobbie Duncan left, McKinney spent the rest of the morning on the couch, in front of the television. Thinking about a man who was vengeful enough to destroy his family's home had soured his mood even more than usual. He was watching a TV court show when his mother came in from the kitchen and switched off the television.

"Hey," McKinney said. "I was watching that. A woman was suing her landlord to get her security deposit back, but all the judge wanted to hear about was why she installed a stripper pole in the living room…"

She ignored him. "Why don't you quit moping around and take us all to lunch? Jill and Angelina could use a little diversion."

"I'm sorry, Mom. I'm just not very good company today. How about if I take us all out for dinner?"

"You need to get off your rump, honey. Those two girls had a frightening experience yesterday and…"

Angelina scurried in, interrupting. "We want to go to the grocery store to get cleaning supplies so we can start fixing up Jill's house. Can somebody drive us?" She looked at her father. "Dad…"

"I've got all the supplies you girls need," her grandmother said. "I'll get them together for you, and I'll give you some garbage bags to put the broken stuff in. Besides, your father might not want to go to the grocery store. He might be embarrassed." She winked at Angelina.

"Oh, Mom," McKinney said. "Not this story again."

"It seems," she said, taking Angelina's hand, "that when you were a very little girl, you occasionally threw temper tantrums. One time, when you and your mom and dad were at the grocery store, you lay down on the floor and started screaming and kicking your feet because they wouldn't buy you any candy. Well, your mother was always full of creative solutions. She lay down next to you and started screaming and kicking her feet, too. You were so surprised you stopped crying and sat right up."

"And I was so embarrassed I moved back about twenty feet to watch," McKinney said.

"Your mother took advantage of your dad's bashfulness. She picked you up and followed him around the store saying things like, "Please darling, don't throw us out into the cold" and "Deny us if you will, Clarence, the child is yours." Your mother had a marvelous sense of humor."

Angelina threw her head back and laughed. She laughed until her sides hurt. She wiped away tears that were equal parts joy and sorrow. "Ha!" she said. "Mom owned you, Dad."

"Yes," he said. "Yes she did."

○

McKinney woke from a dream about his wife and daughter. He had dreamt of Catherine, following him around a store saying, "Deny us if you will." He was still on the living room couch, and the glare from the television lit the dim room. He looked at the balcony doors. It was dusk. A noise from the kitchen caught his attention. "Mom?" he called.

She came in, wiping her hands on a dishtowel. "Have a nice nap?" she asked.

"Yeah." He stretched and stood up. "Are the girls here? It looks like it's almost time for dinner."

"They're still across the street. I was just about to call

over there."

McKinney walked to the balcony doors and looked out. Across the street, parked in front of the Duncan's house, sat a red pickup truck. McKinney shoved his feet into his shoes and headed for the front door. "Call the police," he shouted. "Tell them to get over here, now."

He slid to a stop at the front door to the Duncan house and tried the knob. The door was locked. He plowed through the snow, cutting across the yard to the back door. It was no longer boarded shut, but when he pushed, the door only opened an inch or so. He looked through the kitchen window. The refrigerator had been toppled onto its side and shoved against the door. McKinney grabbed a lawn chair from the patio, shook the snow off, and used it to shatter the kitchen window. He ran the chair along the sill, clearing away the sharp edges, and climbed through into the dark kitchen. There was no point in being quiet. If Duncan was here he would have heard the breaking glass. McKinney called out. "Bella! Jill!" No answer. He crept through the kitchen to the hallway, trying to avoid stepping on broken glass, listening. A voice he didn't recognize said, "In the living room, buddy. Join the party."

The lights were off in the living room, too, but the drapes were open, and a streetlight lit up the room, glowing yellow and casting long shadows. Angelina and Jill were huddled together on the shredded remains of the couch. Jill cradled Big Bob in her arms. Both girls looked at McKinney as he entered, their eyes big, and fearful in the gloom. A man in a leather coat was crouched on the floor by the window, his back against the wall, his arms resting on his knees. Light coming through the window shone off his bald head. A large, black automatic dangled from his right hand, and sitting next to him was a steel jerry can. McKinney could smell the gasoline.

"This is Mr. Duncan, Dad," Angelina said.

The man waved his gun at McKinney. "Sit your ass down."

McKinney sat. "Duncan," he said. "What's going on?"

"Just waitin' for the missus to get home." He tapped the jerry can with the barrel of his gun. "Gonna have a little bar-be-cue."

The man's voice quavered. This guy is on the edge, McKinney thought. He glanced out the window. How long since his mother called the police? Would their presence help, or would it set this guy off?

"Whatever you want to do," McKinney said. "But let's get the girls out of here first. Look at them—they're scared to death."

"No can do, buddy. I like the company."

"For what? You going to burn the house down?"

"That's likely to be the result," Duncan said, "but this can of gas is for me. Bitch destroys my life, let's see if she can live with my death."

Jill began to cry. She squeezed Big Bob, and he let out a yip. Angelina put her arms around them both. "But you can't..." she started.

McKinney cut her off. "Don't say anything, Bella."

"Smart man," Duncan said. "Maybe you should all keep your mouths shut."

"I just figure pleading with you is a waste of time. Anyone willing to do what you're planning is too egotistical and selfish to reason with."

Duncan raised the gun and sighted down the barrel at McKinney. "Don't push it, pal. You can't manipulate me with your little games. You're not smart enough. Hell, Bobbie's the selfish one." He sat back and smoothly spun the gun on his index finger. McKinney pictured him practicing fast draws and fancy tricks in front of a mirror.

"Would she subject Jill to the kind of horror you're planning?" McKinney asked.

"I thought I told you to shut the hell up."

"I'm a father, too," McKinney said. "I know what I'm talking about. Jill is the miracle you helped create. She's your gift to the world." He stood up and inched slowly forward. "Being a father doesn't give you the right to terrorize her. It means accepting your responsibility to help her and to love her, no matter what, for the rest of your life."

"Which isn't going to be much longer for either of us if you don't sit back down." He pointed the gun at McKinney's stomach. McKinney sat down. He was closer to the man, but not much.

Duncan looked at him, hard. "I will god damn kill you if you try that again. This is my last day on earth, and I don't intend to let you mess with me. The only woman I ever loved betrayed me. She caused me so much pain that I just plain don't want to be in this world anymore, and she is going to watch me leave it. You can't possibly understand how I feel, so you can shove your punk-ass psychology or whatever else you think you wanna try."

McKinney laughed. He laughed a little too long and saw the girls looking at him and realized that his laughter must sound crazy. He looked down at his hands, clenching them in his lap. "Duncan," he said, "my wife died last year. She had a cancer that devoured her, and all I could do was watch. I watched her light grow dimmer and dimmer, and when it went out I felt like my light had gone out, too. And you know what? That's when my daughter needed me the most, and I failed her. You and I do have something in common, we're fathers. Everything that word signifies was planted in us, like a seed, when our girls were born. It may be the only part of us that's worth anything." He looked up at the man holding the gun. "We have no right to indulge our grief."

It was quiet after that. McKinney strained to hear approaching sirens. The only sound was Jill, quietly weeping. She looked at her father. "Daddy?" she said.

Tires crunched through the frozen snow out in the street. Cold, blue lights stabbed into the room, illuminating Duncan's tortured face. His eyes were wet. McKinney felt the dampness on his own cheeks. Duncan stood and walked to the door. He looked back at his daughter. When he spoke his voice was subdued. "I'm sorry, Cupcake," he said. He tossed McKinney the gun and stepped out into the flashing lights.

○

It was Friday afternoon in a cold Chicago February, and McKinney was just finishing up a report on a gun shot residue case when his telephone rang. The case had only come into the lab the previous afternoon, but it was high priority, and his supervisor asked him to work it right away—another drive-by shooting, another innocent bystander killed. The media was all over it. He hoped the ringing phone wasn't a reporter. He reached through the stacks of books and papers on his desk and reluctantly picked it up.

"McKinney here."

"Hello, honey," his mother said. "Guess who I just spoke with?"

"Hi, Mom. I don't know, Aunt Opal?"

"Sean, your Aunt Opal has been dead for eight years. Try to keep up, dear."

"Okay, I give up. Who did you just speak with?"

"My widow friend, the one whose husband was killed in the hit and run."

"So what happened?" McKinney asked. "Did they catch the driver?"

"They did," she said. "You were right about the car's bumper. The crime lab here was able to match it to the piece of plastic from the crime scene. When her detective friend confronted the owner of the car with the evidence, he confessed. My friend says 'thank you,' and she'll take us all to dinner the next time you come up to visit."

"That's great. Ask her to keep my participation quiet, though. There's a four-inch thick binder in my supervisor's office titled Illinois State Police Forensic Science Center Rules Of Conduct. I'm sure giving out advice must have violated at least one of them."

"Sure, honey. And how's my favorite granddaughter?"

"She's fine. I'm taking her out to Starved Rock State Park tomorrow. There's a little canyon Catherine and I used to go to in the winter. Icicles from the waterfall at the top hang down almost to the canyon floor, about 40 feet. It looks like a ballroom for elves. I want her to see it before the ice melts."

"She'll be able to see the wildflowers out there in a couple of months," his mother said. "Spring will be here before you know it."

McKinney looked out the window at the snow-covered parking lot and the barren trees. "Not a moment too soon," he said.

DIRTY WATER

    I'm not sure how long I've been drifting. Two days? Maybe three? The storm kicked up again after I left the old man, and I lost the oars when I tried to bring them aboard. They were awkward, and the wind ripped them out of my hands. It's sunny today. I'm just lying here, looking up at the sky through my fingers. The sun is strong behind them, and it makes my flesh translucent. I can see all the little bones in my hand. My sunburn is starting to bother me again, so I should probably sit up and try to get my bearings or at least turn over. I'd rather just lie here, though, and watch the clouds.

    Sitting up disturbs me. Yesterday I saw a corpse floating face down in the water. Its long black hair was streaming out behind it, rippling in the current. I couldn't tell if it had been a man or a woman. It was swollen with gas and looked like it was ready to pop. When I lay back down in the boat I could see people walking across a bridge. It looked like they were singing or something. I tried to shout "Hey!" up to them but my throat was horse, and my cracked lips started bleeding again. I drank a little of the rainwater that had collected on the bottom of the boat. It tasted dirty, and I almost threw it up. The street signs were still under water, and I didn't recognize the bridge. No familiar landmarks. I figured sooner or later the Mississippi would carry the flood back out to the gulf, and this little skiff would set down on a mud bank. Then I could figure my location and head for home.

Earlier today, I started picking at the green paint peeling off the inside of the boat. I had a nice pile of paint chips going, but I cracked a fingernail, so I had to stop. Guess I was too enthusiastic. This afternoon I've been drifting in and out of sleep. Fragments of memory enter my consciousness and then, float away.

I remember lying in another boat on a hot August day. We're in under the cypress, so there's plenty of shade, and a breeze keeps the mosquitoes off. I'm in the bow, eating cold fried chicken and drinking Pepsi from a bottle. My fingers smell like bait, but I don't care. My father is sitting in the stern, talking to my mother and handling the tiller. They think I'm not paying attention, but I am. He's worried about money. We're drifting slow, and I can see that my mother has a fish on her line, but they both ignore it. The line cuts back and forth through the water, taut, the bobber submerged.

Then, I'm coming in late from school, expecting to get a whupping, but instead I find my mother sitting alone at the kitchen table, crying. I had thrown the screen door wide behind me, and it slams shut, startling me just as I see her.

Now, I'm sitting in a hot courtroom on a hard bench, my mother telling me to stop fidgeting. My shirt collar is so stiff I imagine it slicing my throat from ear to ear. I hate dressing up, and I try not to move inside my itchy shirt and pants, positioning my limbs so the material doesn't touch my skin. A big man with a strawberry mark on his face points at my father, who is sitting just ahead of us at a table with another man. The strawberry mark is shaped like a palm print and it looks hot, like the devil had slapped the man across his face. The man shouts at the jury, telling them lies about my father. Calling my father a killer.

I found this boat drifting, empty, soon after the first levee broke. I knew where I was then, of course. And I knew where the old man was. He wasn't far. He was right over in the nursing home on Josephine Street. I've stayed close to him since that day five years ago when I learned about Robert Henry. My wife and I argued about taking the apartment near the nursing home. She didn't see the point. Just as well. I couldn't have taken advantage of this opportunity if we were still together.

I believe in the law. No one has come up with a better way for people to live together without destroying one another. I also believe that retribution weakens society, and it damages the soul. Jesus tried to save us from that particular hell. No more eye-for-an-eye, he said. Try turning the other cheek. I tried.

When I got to the nursing home there were rescue workers there already. They were helping the sick and elderly residents into two boats, police boats with outboard motors. One of the officers was wearing a bright orange life jacket. He waved at me as I rowed past. I piloted my commandeered skiff around the back, tied it to the frame of a broken window, and climbed through. The electricity was out, but there was enough light coming in from the windows to give the rooms and corridors a twilight luminance. The old man's room was on the second floor. I knew this from my last visit.

I took the fire stairs up, two at a time, trying to beat the rescue workers. I needn't have hurried. He was sitting by himself in a wheel chair at the end of the hall. His gnarled hands ran back and forth along the edges of the shoebox on his lap.

"Counselor Dewitt," I called. He turned his head and smiled up at me. His voice quavered when he spoke.

"I thought y'all had about forgot me," he said. "Missus Bonnard said she'd come right back for me, but I couldn't help fretting."

"We're going right now, Counselor Dewitt." I released the brake on his chair and started to push him back down the hall, the way I'd come.

"Them others took the main stairs," he said.

"Well sir, my boat's out back." I tried to make my voice soft and comforting. "You just leave everything to me. We'll have you high and dry in no time. High and dry."

I took him down the stairs, lowering the chair down step after step, one at a time. He didn't weigh much, nowhere near what he'd weighed that first time I saw him, but it was still a tough job. He let out a little gasp each time the wheels bumped on a step. I was drenched in sweat by the time we got to the bottom.

"That was quite a ride, young man."

"Well, we're down," I said. "Not much further, now." There was water on the floor almost up to my knees, and it ran in a slow current down the hall. I struggled to push open the door to the room I had first come through and wheeled the chair in backwards, sloshing through the water and getting us both wet. I parked the chair near the window and put on the brake. There was debris in the water, soda bottles and little hunks of wood and lath—soap scum, too. The muck eddied around his chair, sending out whorls of filth that floated out the door into the hall. Some of them shimmered with little rainbows of motor oil.

"You don't recognize me, do you, sir?" I asked.

"I'm sorry, son. When you get to be my age the memory doesn't work real well. Please don't take it personal."

"I'm Roger Michaud, Claude's boy." The name meant nothing to him. He cocked his head to one side and pursed his lips. I had come to see him a half dozen times over the years, but he didn't remember.

"I'm sorry," he said at last. He flushed a little with embarrassment, making the strawberry mark on his face stand out.

"You knew my daddy a long time ago," I said.

"Well, you give him my regards, and tell him I believe he's raised himself a fine young man." He looked down at the water that was soaking his lap and held the shoebox higher. "We'd best get to your boat, hadn't we?"

"I'm just starting to realize how little I appreciated my father, Counselor Dewitt. I miss him more today than I did when he died. Was killed, I mean. He was killed in prison by a deranged inmate who broke his head open with a table leg."

He looked up at me like he didn't understand what I was telling him. The water had started to pour in over the windowsill. It sounded almost pleasant, like a waterfall. He held his box up to me.

"Please," he said, "my things."

"Of course, I was just a boy when he went to prison. That man loved to fish. He spent most of his time out at his fishing camp. Did you know he loved to fish, Counselor? Why, you must've. You seemed to know all about him at his trial and at his parole hearing. You went on for a good long time about what a danger he was. I seem to recall you said he was a 'horrible menace' or some such thing."

He wasn't paying attention to me. He kept worrying over his shoebox. I took it from his outstretched hands and dumped the contents into the swirling waters. Photographs, letters, everything spread out on the water and started to sink.

"Why...?" he said. I cut him off.

"Don't you remember about Robert Henry, Counselor? I've told you about him. It was only five years ago that he confessed to the murder you sent my father to prison for. There was still evidence from the crime, too. They had kept it in some vault at the Coroner's office. They checked Robert Henry's DNA. It matched. You sent an innocent man to prison." I leaned down to look into his eyes. "His name was Claude Michaud. Do you remember him now?"

He was flailing about, trying to fish his belongings out of the water. He had managed to clutch a couple of soggy pictures and put them in his jacket. He looked at me then, his face twisted in pain.

"I'm sorry," he said.

For a moment I thought that would be enough. I

wanted to drag him into the boat and row him around the front of the building and hand him over to the rescue teams. I wanted it to be enough, but it wasn't.

I climbed out the window into the waiting skiff. There wasn't much time; the water was rising again, flooding in over the sill and filling the room. I slipped and went under, briefly. I pulled myself into the boat. My wet clothes reeked of the dirty water. I untied the boat and used one of the oars to push off from the building. The old man didn't say a word. I sat there in the boat, floating about ten feet from the window and watched. It was getting dark in the room, but I could still see the strawberry mark on his upturned face. Near the end I had to duck way down and peer over the gunnel to keep him in sight. I expected him to howl or scream or beg me to come back. I didn't necessarily want him to, but I expected he would. He just sat there in his wheelchair and cried. His shoulders shook a little. A streak of sunlight glinted off the top of his bald head as the water rose up, lifting him out of the chair, and then the water level was higher than the top of the window, and I couldn't see him anymore. I couldn't see him, but I could still hear him crying. He was crying and moaning, and as the sound got louder I gripped the gunnel so tight my fingers cramped. I tried to relax them, letting go of the wood, rubbing my hands together. Then I realized that the moaning was coming from me. I shut my mouth and tried to wipe the tears off my face with my soaking-wet shirtsleeves. Then there was silence.

This morning I thought I heard some sea birds, and I got excited. Sea birds would mean land and getting off this boat and going home. I was wrong. I sat up and looked, and there was nothing. I turned and stared, shading my eyes from the sun and straining to see clear to the horizon. In every direction was nothing but the awfulness of water, stretched out before me like a slowly heaving prairie. The only sound was the gentle rhythm of water against the sides of the boat. It was too horrible. I lay back down and closed my eyes.

　　I hardly feel the motion of the boat now, especially when I squeeze my eyes tight shut. It almost feels like the boat has stopped moving. Like the boat and I are stationary, and it's the world that keeps rising and falling under us.

EASY PIECE

I think Clark heard the screaming first. We were sitting in Rosa's Cafe in the little town of El Rosario, about halfway down the Baja peninsula on the Pacific side. We had been digging fossils up in the hills and were dirty and hungry and tired. It was after ten, and we didn't talk much as we ate the peppers and eggs. Then we heard the scream.

Clark mumbled through a hunk of toast, "Who's screaming?"

"Beats me. Sounds like it's heading this way."

I tried to quench the fire in my mouth with a drink of warm Pepsi. Then the door banged open, and the Fat American staggered in. The front of his shirt was red and wet, and he stood there and looked around the room. He looked at us, and his mouth opened and closed a few times like a fish out of water. Then he fell over and died. I knelt beside him and put my finger on the side of his neck. There was no pulse, and the blood had stopped oozing from the little holes in his chest. A woman appeared in the doorway and started screaming. I guess she was the one we had heard scream before.

The Fat American arrived yesterday, just after dark. Clark and I had been drinking beer and talking with some of the locals outside under the only streetlight in town. There was a card game going on, and some kids were playing catch with a baseball that had lost its cover. There were a half dozen stray dogs hovering around, sniffing for scraps. We had come down looking for turquoise, but they were having a little war down there, and we didn't think it was worth getting shot at. A lot of other Americans had heard about the turquoise mines, and the Mexican government had heard about the Americans. I guess they figured that if there were Americans involved there was money to be had. They sent some Federales down to take the land away from the people who had lived on it for generations so it could be leased to the American miners. You could get a twenty-year lease for a hundred dollars a year. If your mine produced that meant a hefty profit. The only trouble was that the guy who had originally owned the land didn't get squat, and he was probably going to be pissed about it. We decided to go up into the hills and dig for fossils instead. It turned out that the locals, who were mostly fishermen, and the Federales didn't think it was worth getting shot at either. During the day they would go out into the desert and fire off a few rounds, and then meet back in town after dinner for cards and beer. It was a very civilized war. When we told them that we didn't want a land lease they decided we were okay and let us get drunk with them. One of the men, Alfredo, spoke English. He translated for us. Sometimes he'd add a little joke at our expense to amuse the fishermen, but since they all had guns that was all right with me.

    We saw the big yellow Cadillac coming, lurching

along the ruts of the dirt road. Its headlights were winking on and off, and it kicked up a trail of dust behind it. It pulled up a few feet from our card game. The engine chugged a few times and quit. Then the Fat American got out.

"Where's the gas station around here?" he asked.

"Rosa has a tank out behind the cafe." Alfredo gestured with his thumb.

"Is there a mechanic? Something's wrong with my car."

Alfredo got up and walked over to the car. "I'm a mechanic," he said. "What's the problem?"

Alfredo, we had learned, had an interesting occupation. He was a traveling mechanic. He would drive the length of the peninsula from Tijuana to La Paz fixing cars. After each trip he'd spend a few days with his family. While he and the Fat American were looking under the hood of the Cadillac the rest of us went back to playing cards. Suddenly, we heard a squeal, and a woman jumped out of the Cadillac and started hopping up and down.

"A dog! Daddy, there's a dirty old dog in the car! A dog! A dog!"

The Fat American had left his car door open, and one of the stray dogs had jumped in. The woman was a pneumatic blonde who was fighting off middle age with bright red lipstick, a short lavender dress, and matching pumps. The Fat American looked in the car. He took out a handkerchief and wiped the sweat off his neck.

"Whose dog is this?" His tone was imperious. "Come on, who owns this filthy dog? Get him out of my car. Now!"

I looked over at Clark. He rolled his eyes.

"It's a stray," I said. "It doesn't belong to anyone."

The woman quit hopping up and down and looked in the car. "He's eating the sandwiches, Daddy! Oh, hell. He's eating all the sandwiches."

Alfredo reached in and pulled the dog out of the car. The dog took his sandwich and ran under a parked car. Alfredo turned to the Fat American.

"You need a new alternator. I can go to Ensanada tomorrow and pick one up for you."

"How long will that take?"

"A day. I'll have you back on the road by day after tomorrow."

The woman came trotting over. "But Daddy, where are we gonna stay?" She looked like she was about to cry. "That dog ate all the ham. All that's left is tuna."

"Don't worry honey. We'll be fine."

"But I don't like tuna."

He patted her on the rump and turned to Alfredo. "How far is El Rosario?"

"This is El Rosario, señior."

The Fat American looked surprised. "Well hell. I thought there'd be more to it than this. Where's the hotel?"

"There is no hotel, but I know a woman who will rent you her spare room. It's very clean."

The Fat American looked at the broken-down Cadillac and sighed. "All right. Where is it?"

Alfredo helped him carry the luggage, and they walked off into the night with the blonde whimpering along behind them.

o

The raindrops were huge. They made a plopping noise on the tent and a pinging noise on the hood of the jeep. Clark had gotten up before me and made coffee. I poured myself a cup and walked down to the beach. He was sitting under a sandstone outcropping watching the turbulent water. The Pacific was pretty violent, and I could see a storm front moving in.

"Sleep well?" he asked.

"Yeah. Thanks for the coffee."

"Looks like it may get too wet to dig today."

"Maybe we can find that cave."

Rosa had a little display case in the cafe that contained a few big turquoise nuggets and some fossils. In front of the display case were two incredible finds: a fossilized chambered nautilus shell the size of an automobile tire and a carved, stone head. A rainstorm, she said, had uncovered the fossil. The stone head was part of a trade she had made with a local Indian. He claimed that he had found it in a nearby cave that contained several other pieces. It was definitely pre-Columbian.

"The only way we're going to find that cave," I said, "is if Rosa introduces us to the Indian who found the head."

Clark shrugged. "That isn't very likely. She claims that some professor from Los Angeles offered her ten thousand dollars American for it. He's supposed to come back with a check from the museum."

A couple of raindrops plopped into my coffee cup.

"You don't suppose that guy in the Cadillac is him?"

"You're kidding."

"Well, he's either a college professor or a used car

salesman."

"What's the difference?"

"A salesman has better taste in clothes."

The storm, just offshore, started to move parallel to the coastline. I pointed to the patch of blue sky that was starting to open up. "Looks like we may get to do some digging after all."

Clark looked thoughtful. "What the hell do you suppose that guy's doing down here, driving a Caddy on dirt roads?"

"You mean besides being a jerk to the locals?"

"Exactly. A guy like that is used to getting what he wants. Why would he come to a backward little place like El Rosario?"

"Maybe he heard about the turquoise."

"Right. I can just see him and the blonde digging and sifting."

I shrugged. "He looks like a money guy to me. You know, horses, dope, smuggling, whatever. A guy like that wouldn't do his own digging, but he'd want to check things out."

"I'd hate to think that he came down here for the turquoise. I mean, that's why we came down here."

"Everybody's greedy to some extent, Clark. It's just a matter of degree. Some guys don't mind stepping on a few people while they rake it in."

I dumped the rest of my coffee on the sand and stood up. "Let's go find some fossils."

o

Rosa came out of the back room and stared at the

screaming blonde. Then she saw the corpse on the floor. A couple of Federales pushed past the woman in the doorway. They saw the body on the floor too and started talking very fast. My Spanglish wasn't much use, and I wished that Alfredo was there to translate. One of the men was talking to me, and when I didn't answer him he took his gun out of its holster and started waving it around. Clark turned pale, and the blonde stopped screaming. Rosa decided to help out.

"He wants to know if you knew the dead man."

I turned to Rosa. "Thank you. Tell him that the woman is the only one who knows him."

She told him. The blonde looked at me and started to cry. "Marty and I were going to get married," she sobbed. "See."

She held up her left hand. The diamond on her third finger was as big as a robin's egg. The Federale with the gun said something to Rosa.

"He says that you and your friend should go outside. They want to talk with the woman."

"Thanks," I said. I picked up my last piece of toast and stepped over a puddle of Marty's blood into the night.

○

I was awakened by the most noxious odor I had ever smelled. It was a little after dawn, and when I crawled out of my tent the sand still held the rosy glow of sunrise. I tossed a few pebbles at Clark's tent.

"Cut it out. I'm up." He crawled out holding his nose. "What died?"

We walked down to the beach. A dead whale had washed ashore during the night. It looked like it had been dead for some time. It was covered with more flies and birds than I'd ever seen in one place before. I tossed a pebble at the whale. It bounced straight up in the air and startled a dozen or so gulls. Clark looked disgusted.

"That's it," he said. " I'm ready to go home."

"Home? What for? Things are just getting interesting."

"Interesting for you maybe, but I run a hardware store. We've got a land war, a murder, a dead whale and no turquoise. I'm through."

Clark was right. The time I had spent as an operative for the West Coast Detective Agency had left me with a rather macabre sense of curiosity.

"We've got some nice fossils," I said. "The rock shop in La Jolla will give us twenty bucks apiece for the large trilobites."

"Whoop-de-doo."

"Come on, Clark. Let's stay one more day. I want to have a talk with that blonde if the Federales haven't carted her off. I'm curious about who killed Fat American."

"You mean Marty."

"Yeah. You can drop me off in town on your way to the fossil fields."

Clark sighed. "You're nuts. All right, on one condition."

"What's that?"

"We move camp up the beach. The smell of that whale is making me sick."

Clark let me out at the cafe, and I went inside to find Rosa. She was behind the counter. The blonde was sitting at one of the tables looking very uncomfortable. A Federale with medals on his shirt was sitting across from her. Rosa smiled when I came in.

"Señior, this is Captain Mendez. He was asking for you. He has English."

The Federale motioned to a chair. I sat down.

"Miss Samsa says that you were here last night when her friend was killed."

"I was here when he died."

The blonde let out a sob. "Poor Marty!"

"I'm sorry Miss..."

"Samsa. Doris Samsa." She held out her hand, and I took it.

"I'm sure Captain Mendez asked you already, Doris, but what happened?" I looked at the Federale to see if he had any objections to my questioning his witness. He just looked at the blonde and nodded. She started biting the paint off a thumbnail.

"Well, I was hungry, and all we had left was tuna sandwiches on account of that dog. Marty saw the lights on in the cafe, so we started to walk over from where we were staying. I heard a popping noise, and then Marty grabbed his chest and started running. I followed him, and he ran in here. Then he fell down." She looked at her thumbnail. "We were gonna be married."

"Did you see anyone else?"

"No. It was dark."

Captain Mendez got up and walked around the table. He took the blonde's elbow and escorted her to the door. "Please wait for me outside, Senorita. I will be with you in a moment."

The blonde picked up her handbag and went outside. Captain Mendez came back to the table.

"She's lying, of course."

"You think she killed him?" I asked.

"Either that or she knows who did. Did you see the dead man's shirt?"

"Not close up. He fell on his stomach."

"There were singe marks. He was shot at a very close range."

"You're not just a soldier, are you?" I asked.

"I used to be a police officer in Mexico City."

"Did you swab her hands for gunshot residue?"

"No. Perez was in charge last night. She had all night to wash it off her hands."

"So why did she lie?"

"I'm hoping that you can help me answer that question. You and your friend have been here for several days. Have you met any of the other Americans?"

"Not to speak to. We've mostly stayed away from the mines."

"There are some Americans here who do not dig for turquoise. They say that they are here because they no longer enjoy living in the city. We think that some of them are buying drugs to smuggle back into the U.S." He gave me a dour look. "Are you buying drugs?"

"No. This would be a good place for it, though. The drugs could come in by boat, and the mule could drive down from L.A. to pick them up. The border police at Tijuana are mostly looking for illegals. They probably wouldn't pay much attention to a guy like Marty."

"That's what I think too. Maybe this time someone got greedy."

"But how can I help? I don't know anybody here. Anyway, all you have to do is wait until Doris is ready to leave town and search that big, old Cadillac."

"I don't care about the drugs, señior, but I can't have you Americans coming down here and killing each other. We've had this little war here for eight months, and the worst injury so far is a man who got drunk and fell into a ditch. He broke his arm. If Americans start dying here it will attract the attention of my superiors, and they will tell the politicians and we will all have trouble. Talk to this Doris. Help her prepare to go back to Los Angeles, and let me know if anyone else contacts her."

"You don't think the drugs are already in the car?"

"I know Alfredo. He wouldn't fix Señior Marty's car without telling me."

"I promised my friend that we'd head for home tomorrow. I'll spend the rest of today with her. Where can I find you if something comes up?"

"Rosa has been kind enough to allow me to use this cafe as my office." He stood up and held out his hand. "Thank you, señior. Try not to get shot."

It was just mid-morning, but it was already hot. Doris was standing in a patch of shade under a small scrub pine. She was fiddling with her engagement ring, and there were beads of perspiration on her upper lip.

"What did he say?"

"Captain Mendez asked me to help you make

arrangements to take Marty back to the States."

"Oh, yes. He gave me this phone number. It's a mortuary in Ensanada. They'll pick up Marty and ship him to L.A."

I took the slip of paper she was holding. "Let's give them a call. Then we'll walk over and see if Alfredo's got your car running."

The man at the mortuary spoke a little English, which made my job easier. He said that he'd send someone to pick up Marty tomorrow and that we should keep him cool in the meantime. That was going to be difficult in a town with no ice. Since there was a nice breeze blowing, we laid him in the shade and covered him with a damp sheet. Doris was quiet through most of this. She played with her ring and sniffled a lot. Finally we walked over to where Alfredo was working on the Cadillac. A pair of sneakers on the end of a pair of legs was protruding from under the car. I tapped one with my foot.

"Alfredo?"

"Damn! Just a minute." Alfredo crawled out from under the car. He pulled a rag out of a back pocket and smeared the grease on his hands around a little. He looked at Doris. "I'm sorry about your friend, Miss."

Doris started crying again. She showed Alfredo her ring. "We were gonna be married."

I motioned toward the car. "How's it coming?"

"A couple of hours. The old alternator's rusted in place. I need to look in my trunk for the extension to this wrench."

Doris and I walked back toward the cafe. It was late

in the afternoon, and the long shadows from the houses made oblong patterns in the red dirt streets. It was starting to look like no one was going to approach Doris while I was with her. I watched her out of the corner of my eye. Patches of light and dark passed across her face as we walked. She seemed sad but not particularly anxious. Maybe Captain Mendez had been mistaken. Maybe she was telling the truth. I decided to try a more direct approach.

"So, why did you and Marty come to El Rosario?"

"Marty was a jewelry wholesaler. He knew a guy down here who's got a mine. He was going to buy a bunch of turquoise cheap and get one of his regulars to polish it up for him."

"Did he meet with him?"

"No. He was k-k-killed before..." She started to sniffle again. She stopped and turned her back to me as she opened her purse to fish out a tissue.

"So when was the wedding going to be?"

She stopped crying and turned to face me. Her eyes were a little unfocused, and her mouth twisted into an angry shape. "Why are you asking me all these questions?" she shouted.

"Just trying to make conversation. I didn't mean to pry."

"I loved Marty. I did everything for him." Her voice started to get louder. "I wanted to spend the rest of my life with him, but he wouldn't leave her! He promised me that he'd divorce her, and I believed him. He never even told her! The bitch didn't even know I existed until I called her."

She took a step backward. Her hand was still in her

purse. The words were coming faster now. She sprayed saliva as she talked, like she couldn't get the words out fast enough. "He always took me on his buying trips. He was mad at me for telling her. He said this was our last trip together. I was going to spend the rest of my life with him, and all this time I was just his easy piece. That's what he told me, that I was his easy piece."

She stopped and stood there, panting. She looked down at her feet. I looked too. There was red dust on her lavender pumps.

The next few seconds happened in slow motion. I saw the gun as she pulled it out of her purse. It was a little .25 caliber Beretta. A lady's gun. Her hand started the journey to her temple just as I started to step toward her. I didn't think I was going to make it. It was lucky for both of us that I tripped. I fell against her legs, and she went over backwards. She pulled the trigger when she hit the ground. The bullet whizzed over my head and smacked into the adobe wall of a nearby house. I crawled a few feet and got my hand on her gun. She let me take it. The fall had knocked the wind out if her, and she was gasping for air. Finally she rolled onto her side and lay there, crying softly.

I had no doubt that it was the gun that had killed Marty. She had discovered that the man she loved thought of her as a convenience. I didn't like Marty. I didn't know him, but I didn't like him. Maybe he had kids who thought he was a great guy. Maybe he was a pillar in his community. All I knew about him was that he treated the locals like they were his servants, and he had broken this sad, silly woman's heart. I didn't know her either, but I felt sorry for her. She had murdered a man, and that was wrong by any standard. I touched her shoulder. She shivered a little but kept crying. I thought about throwing the gun in the ocean and keeping my mouth shut. I thought about Marty lying in the shade with a wet sheet over him. I slipped the little Beretta into my pocket and stood up. She looked like a lavender island in the sea of red dirt. I turned and walked away.

Captain Mendez intercepted me outside the cafe.

"So, what have you to tell me?"

I looked down. A large, brown beetle was scurrying through the dust at our feet. "Well, she didn't meet anyone."

The beetle came to a rock. Instead of going around the rock, it started to climb over.

"Señior, sometimes when a person is away from his home things seem very different. Life may appear to be like an amusement park or a fiesta. Our everyday world seems, somehow, remote. At these times a person may not behave in the way that he normally would. He might do something foolish. Do you not agree?"

The beetle slipped off the rock and fell onto its back. It struggled for a second, flailing its legs in the air. I bent down and gave it a push with my finger. It started to climb the rock again. I pulled the little gun out of my pocket and handed it to Captain Mendez.

A BLADE OF GRASS

I never knew a blade of grass contained so many different shades of green—olive, jade, pea soup, emerald, lime, chartreuse, each color distinct. If I squint they kind of blend together, but I can tell that each one is there, different from the others. Why didn't I ever notice that before? And this dirt, it's so varied. Rich brown clumps and sandy powder. What's that shiny bit, a piece of quartz? It's refracting the sunlight. I can actually see a tiny rainbow on the ground next to it. Wait, that's not quartz. It looks more like glass. I bet it's a piece of the windshield. Of course.

º

Here comes an ant. No wonder they use them in monster movies. Those jaw things look like they could do some damage. What's the name again? Mandibles? Wonder what he's going to do with that twig? Funny that I'd call it "he." Is the queen the only female ant? Do all the other ants live to serve her? No that's bees, I think. God, I wish Evelyn was here. What am I saying? No I don't. What if she were injured, or worse? I couldn't live with that. I don't know if I can live with this. I don't hurt. I don't feel anything. I can't believe I'm so calm. Maybe I'm in shock. Dearest Evelyn. She could have any man she wanted. I don't know what she sees in an old codger like me, but whatever it is, I'm glad. She makes me happy. I haven't been this happy since Marie was alive.

o

I wish I could turn onto my back so I could see the sky. There's a little bit of it above that stick. Nice and blue, just the way I like it. Maybe I can at least move my head. Come on, concentrate, move, move, moooove dammit. Shit. Oh shit, I'm screwed. What's that noise? Is that me? It sounds so far away. I guess I'm crying. It sounds funny, like wheezing and something else. Crackling? What's that smell? Burning rubber? Maybe the Bentley is on fire. Hope it doesn't explode.

I hate anti-lock brakes. Didn't Evelyn just have the brakes fixed? Yeah, that mechanic friend of hers worked on them last weekend. I hope he hasn't cashed the check yet because I'm not paying him for a half-assed job like this.

o

Another ant. Is that the same one? How do ants tell each other apart? I wonder if they have names? Hey Stanley, did you catch the mandibles on that babe? He's bending that long blade of grass across that little red river. Oh shit, red river. Is that blood? Where's the fucking ambulance? People drive this route all the time. Someone's bound to see the car, unless it slid down into the ditch. It's burning though, right? They'll see the smoke. Someone must have called on a cell phone. The ambulance is probably on its way.

o

Look at little Stanley move. Each leg moves independent of the rest. It doesn't even look possible. What amazing coordination, and he was smart enough to use a blade of grass as a bridge.

o

That sounds like footsteps. What's going on? Is someone there? It must be the paramedics. Thank God. I can't feel a damn thing. I must be paralyzed. I guess they'll put a neck brace on me before they move me. What are they doing back there? There's a lot of movement, but I can't see anything. There's a foot. Look out; you'll step on Stanley. High heels? Why would a paramedic wear high heels? She's turning me. Shouldn't they put the neck brace on first? Goodbye Stanley. Goodbye blade of grass.

Evelyn? It's Evelyn. Thank God, you found me. Why are you smiling? You must have been worried sick, poor kid. Is that the mechanic? What's he doing here? Whatever damage there is to the Bentley is your fault, buddy, and you'd better believe you're going to pay. Wait. Where are you going, Evelyn? Evelyn? She must be going to call for an ambulance. Hurry back, sweet Evelyn. At least I can see the sky now. Nice and blue. So many different blues, too. You'd think I would have noticed them, over the years.

WHAT WE DO FOR LOVE

Frank Mosley was alone in the little room behind the chapel as he inspected the collection of crutches, photographs and testimonial letters that covered the wood paneled walls. It was early, and he was the church's first visitor of the day. He read the yellowed letters from people who had been cured of arthritis and stomach ailments. He studied faded photographs of grandmothers who were able to use their gnarled hands for the first time in years and children who were walking again after a crippling injury. He fingered the crutches and the discarded artificial limbs, though Frank couldn't imagine that the holy dirt could grow back an arm or a foot.

The church was in a small town in the Sierra Nevada Mountains of California and was well known for the miracle of its sacred earth. People journeyed from all over the world to scoop the healing earth from the hole in the sacristy floor. The hole itself, el posito, was miraculous. Pilgrims came and scooped earth out of the hole all day long, but no matter how much was taken, the next morning el posito was full again.

Frank had driven all through the night from Sausalito to get some of the sacred earth. While he drove he thought about the miracle. It was ridiculous. What sort of person believes in holy dirt? Why would God make such a thing in the first place? If He wanted to heal someone He wouldn't have to fool around with dirt. It was mass hysteria or some kind of mind over matter, the power of positive thinking. The whole thing was probably bullshit, but Frank needed to believe in it. He had tried to imagine a world without Gloria. The idea was too terrible. Frank was kneeling over the little hole, spooning dirt into a plastic, sandwich bag, when Father Leonard tapped him on the shoulder.

"Excuse me, sir," the priest said. "May I have a word with you?"

"Frank stood up and brushed dirt off the knees of his trousers. He was a full head taller than the priest and had to duck as he followed him through the little arched doorway. They walked out a side door, around to the back of the church, and stopped next to a mound of black dirt. The church was on a ridge, and several small houses and trailers dotted the landscape on the mountainside below. Frank offered the priest a cigarette and, when it was refused, lit one himself. It was a crisp, winter morning and the smoke he pulled into his lungs was made sharper by the mountain air. He had bought the pack at a gas station. He hadn't smoked in years, and he thought how upset Gloria would be if she knew. He had quit a lot of things on account of Gloria—smoking, drinking, breaking people's legs. Fortunately, Papa Bennie hadn't been angry when he left the Organization. He'd even offered to pay for Frank and Gloria's wedding.

"My wife has cancer," Frank said. What do I tell her to do with the dirt when I get it home? I mean, how does she use it?"

"Has she started chemotherapy yet?" the priest asked.

"No. She goes in for a radical mastectomy next week. They'll start chemo after that."

"Some people take the dirt home to bathe in, some eat it or put it in liquid to drink, others rub it on their afflicted limbs. I suggest putting a pinch in a cup of tea. Make sure you give it to her before she starts chemotherapy, though. You don't want her to be eating dirt with a suppressed immune system."

"No," Frank said, "I suppose not."

Father Leonard cleared his throat a few times before he spoke again, as though he was trying to decide the best way to phrase a difficult question.

"You don't believe in our sacred earth, do you?"

It was more a statement than a question, and Frank was surprised by its directness. He thought priests were supposed to encourage faith. He took another drag and snapped the cigarette away. It sailed out over the precipice and down.

"No," he admitted. "I think it's pretty much a crock. Why? Do I have to believe to take some dirt?"

"Not at all," the priest said. He motioned toward the mound of dirt. "Take all you like."

Frank picked up a handful from the pile. It was the same color and consistency as the dirt in his sandwich bag.

"This is the same stuff?" he asked. "I thought the hole in the floor miraculously filled with dirt every night."

"I fill it," the priest said, "every night, three hundred and sixty five nights a year for the last seven years. I have it delivered once a week from a local nursery. Twice a week around Christmas, because of the crowds, you know."

"So you don't believe in it either?"

Father Leonard giggled and covered his mouth with the back of his hand. It seemed an inappropriate sound for a priest, and it occurred to Frank that Father Leonard might have started his morning with booze instead of oatmeal. He inched closer and caught the familiar scent of malt.

"What about all the testimonials and discarded crutches on your wall?" he asked.

"I don't know," the priest said. "Maybe those people would have gotten better anyway. Maybe some of them just think they're healed." He stopped speaking and looked around, as though he was afraid of being overheard. "Maybe some stop taking their medicine and get really sick or die. I haven't got a clue."

"That's awful. They'd be better off if they never took the dirt."

"Probably," the priest said.

"Do you tell everyone who comes here about the dirt, I mean, that the replenishment miracle isn't true?"

"No, you're the first. They wouldn't believe me, anyway. The pilgrims who come for the dirt are mostly poor people, uneducated. All of them are desperate for a miracle. Occasionally, college kids stop in. They're usually just curious or think it's funny. I don't often see someone with a Mercedes and a six hundred dollar suit scooping dirt out of the hole."

"How do you know what my suit cost?" Frank felt himself getting angry. "What difference does that make, anyway? Are you saying that only poor people need hope or that you're stupid if you believe in miracles?"

"No. Hey, I'm sorry," Father Leonard said. He pulled a letter from the waistband of his cassock, handed it to Frank and plopped down on the pile of dirt. "Read the last three lines," he said.

Frank read: Daily insulin injections are very hard for a five year-old boy, and we really can't afford them any more. We're so happy that the sacred earth has cured his diabetes. Thank you, Father Leonard, and praise to God.

"It came in yesterday's mail. There's no name or return address," Father Leonard said. "This family has stopped giving their child his insulin, and I don't know how to get in touch with them. Even if I did, what would I say? Take your child to the doctor because it's all a fraud? Give up your faith?" Father Leonard's hand shook as he took the letter back and put it in his pocket. "My life is a lie. I'm going to shut this place down, and if the archdiocese sends in another priest to run things, I'll show this letter to the press."

Frank put his hand in his pocket and felt the bag of dirt. He wanted to explain to the priest what it was like to walk with Gloria after dinner in the cool evening air. How, when she smelled the night-blooming jasmine, she would stop and close her eyes, and how seeing her like that made him feel as though someone had reached into his chest and wrapped a warm, comforting hand around his heart. Gloria was counting on the dirt. What would she think if she saw in the papers that it was a fraud? He couldn't let that happen.

"It doesn't make any difference whether you or I believe in this crap," Frank said. "My wife believes in it. She read an article in some magazine. I'm sorry about the kid with diabetes, but my wife needs this miracle. If you go to the papers..." He looked at the priest, still sitting on the dirt. "Can't you wait awhile before you do anything? Give me six months, please. That's not too much to ask."

"I can't promise that. In fact, going to the papers may be the only way to save this boy's life. If his family hears that the dirt is a fake perhaps they'll get worried and take him to the doctor."

Frank grabbed Father Leonard's sleeve and yanked him to his feet. He felt like punching him, but instead he shook him, hard, hoping the violent action would sober him up. When he released the priest he was embarrassed and couldn't look at him. Instead, he lit another cigarette. He composed himself as he watched the smoke curl away and drift up into the unclouded sky.

"Look, I'm sorry I got rough," Frank said, "but every night I wake up, maybe three or four times, just to stare at her. I can't get back to sleep until I see her move or hear her breathe. I need to know she's there." He reached out a hand to smooth Father Leonard's rumpled cassock, but the priest pushed him away and walked unsteadily back to the church. Frank looked down at his cigarette for a minute, then let out a sigh. He knew what he had to do. He followed the priest inside.

By the time he returned to his car the flames were licking the wood beams above the windows of the old church. By the time he got to the highway it was just a pale glow in the eastern sky.

SEVEN

Her name was Seven, and she was small and graceful and fast. Only a small patch of brown fur on her back and her green eyes broke the shiny uniformity of her blackness. Her Mama had named her Seven. Her brothers and sisters were One through Fourteen. Mama had said it was just easier that way. She and Five were inseparable. Five was a tiger striped tom with one ear that wouldn't stand up. It had been injured in a fight.

Seven was faster than Five, and sometimes she would hide pieces of the mice or birds she caught where she knew he'd find them. One time, when they were small, he stepped on his own whiskers while stalking a bird. He fell on his face, and the bird looked at him like it was thinking, *Idiot*. She worried about him because he was a little clumsy and because he took foolish chances. She would never admit it, but that was part of why she liked him, too. Everything was a game to him, and he wasn't afraid of anything, not even the men.

Mama had told them about the men. Some of them would give you food, but it was dangerous to go near any of them. They couldn't be trusted. The worst man in the neighborhood was the one with the blue machine. He was big and had no fur on his head, and once he had chased Mama with the machine. She had crossed the street and was on the curb when the machine came right up after her. She jumped aside, but it almost got her, and she heard the man laughing as it zoomed off down the street. After that Mama made them hide whenever she saw the blue machine.

Last week the blue machine hit Five. He and Seven had been hunting in the yard with the bird feeder. Seven was stretched out under a rose bush. The sun was hot, but there was a breeze. It moved her whiskers as it blew. The earth near her twitching nostrils smelled dark and rich and she wasn't really interested in the chattering birds. She was happy to lie there and watch Five stalk them. It was like watching a piece of herself.

Seven heard the door to the house open, and then the dog was there, snarling and slobbering and trying to decide which one to chase. Five and Seven rocketed past him, sailed over the gate, and sprinted up the gangway to the street. Seven was in the lead, and as she crossed the street she saw the blue machine at the end of the block. She called to Five, but it was too late. He was in the street, and the man had seen him. The blue machine was fast. Five darted up a driveway, heading for a tree, but the blue machine followed him. Seven screamed when she saw him disappear under the tire. She ran after it, but the blue machine kept going, down the street and around a corner.

Five was dead. Seven lie down next to him and cried. She lay there all afternoon and all night, and the next day, around mid-day, some men came with a shovel and took Five away. Seven hid while the men were there, and when they left she went looking for the blue machine. It was sitting two blocks over, in the street by the curb, when she found it. She took note of which way its eyes were facing and walked in that direction to the end of the block. Then she crawled under a bush and lie down to wait.

It was dark and wet when she finally saw the man. It had been raining all evening, and she was glad, it would make her job easier. She got up, stretched, and walked out from under the bush, into the middle of the yard. She looked up at the night sky, and the cool rain felt good on her face. The grass was wet, and she was a little worried about slipping, but this was her chance, and she needed to take it. She looked at the man and screamed. He turned toward her, and when she knew he had seen her, she walked out into the middle of the street and sat down.

The blue machine roared as it came to life, and its eyes shone with an evil brightness that bathed the wet street and almost blinded her. She lowered her head to shield her eyes from the glare, and as the machine came toward her she growled, low, deep in her throat. By the time she turned to run the machine was a blue blur, a juggernaut of inevitability, bearing down on her. She cut right at the last moment, and the machine followed her up over the curb and into the fire hydrant. The blue beast caught Seven on its bumper and threw her high over its head, then slammed to a halt as if an invisible hand had grabbed it in mid-lunge.

Seven landed on the wet grass and slid across the lawn, coming to rest next to a tree. She lay still, breathing hard, and listened for the sound of the man's laugh, but all she could hear was the rain and her own heart, pounding in her chest. When she got up everything hurt, and one leg wouldn't work. She limped over to the silent machine and looked up. The man was laying on the hood, half in the machine and half out. His face was covered with blood, and he made little noises, like he was trying to say something but couldn't. There was a pool of water flowing out from under the machine, and Seven looked down at her reflection. A spot of blood stained her head where an ear was torn, and the ear flopped down to one side. It looked a little like Five's ear, and she knew that it would probably heal in that position.

She heard men opening doors and coming out of their houses. She took one last look at the machine and limped off into the night.

KIDDIELAND

The second to the last time I saw Robert Teague Junior alive was the day my mother decided to hand dye the living room carpet. Bobby was a kid I would never have chosen to play with except that our families were close, so we saw a lot of one another. It wasn't because he was boring and spoiled, a lot of kids in the sixth grade were like that, but Bobby was sneaky. If you didn't keep an eye on him he'd pull some stunt, and if it backfired he'd try to blame it on you. He was in my class at Eldridge Elementary because he had been kicked out of several private schools, including the local military academy. "Those boys are just playin' soldier," he liked to say. "Most of 'em wouldn't know their ass from a teacup." The kids in my class were wise to him; he hardly had any friends.

Even though she was just dropping us off, my mother put on a sundress and makeup and fixed her hair. She put my sister in her blue shift; the one she said made Meg's eyes the color of cornflowers. It was a long ride across town from our little red ranch to the Teagues' house, but I enjoyed it. It was a hot day, so I hung my head out the window like a dog, to catch the breeze. The air was moist and heavy and smelled green. It was a cicada year, and their drone was relentless. Every few blocks we'd drive through a cloud of them, turning a couple dozen to paste under the wheels of our old Buick, and I'd have to pull my head in to keep from getting one in my mouth. Meg was curled up, napping, on the back seat. When we pulled into the long driveway leading back through the elms to the Teagues' house my mother snapped at me. "Get your head in here and sit up straight. And brush the hair out of your eyes; you look like a beatnik. Megan, honey, wake up. We're almost there."

My father and Mr. Teague had been in the army together, an experience that made them friends for life. The way they talked about it you'd think they'd won the war by themselves, killing "Krauts" and "keeping Rommel on the run." When they came home from Africa Mr. Teague took over his family's Cadillac dealership. My father went to work on the night shift at the tool and die company. The difference didn't seem to bother the two men, but my mother was very aware that, compared to us, the Teague's were rich.

"Now, don't do anything to embarrass me this time," she said, pulling up in front of the pillared porch at the end of the circular drive. "And eat whatever Dolores gives you for lunch," she looked hard at my sister, "whether you like it or not."

Bobby was sitting on the steps, waiting for us, and he pushed himself to his feet and walked ahead of us to the door. "Let's go," he said. "Mom didn't want to start fixing lunch until you guys got here." The front door was enormous and had a brass knocker shaped like a lion's head. Bobby pushed the door open with his butt and bowed low to let us enter.

We marched Meg down the hallway to the big, sunny kitchen where Bobby's mom was standing at the counter, stirring something in a mixing bowl. She didn't look like anybody's mother; she looked like Princess Grace. She wore slacks and a silk shirt, open at the throat. She was cool and lean and I had to look away to avoid staring at her.

At last, I said, "Hi, Mrs. Teague. We're here."

"Well, if it isn't Bryan and Margaret." She stopped stirring long enough to click off the little radio sitting on the kitchen counter. "I'm just starting a batch of cookies for us to enjoy after we have some lunch. Margaret, why don't you come over here and give me a hand. We'll let the boys go play their boy games." She looked at Bobby. "Lunch in an hour, dear. I'll call you when we're ready."

I looked at Meg. She hated the name Margaret and usually barked at anyone who made the mistake of calling her that. She'd been sent home from school last year for punching a boy who called her Margaret. She'd broken his nose. I saw a scowl slide across her face and disappear. She walked over to Mrs. Teague, looking up at her, reverently, as she went.

Bobby elbowed me in the ribs. "C'mon," he said. "I've got stuff to show you."

We went upstairs to Bobby's room. It was twice as big as the room Meg and I shared, and I wandered around, checking out his toys and looking at all the clothes in his walk-in closet. "Why do you have all these suit coats?" I asked. I turned and saw Bobby across the room, on his hands and knees, pulling something out from under the bed.

"I dunno," he said. "I never wear them. C'mere. Take a gander at this."

He pushed a red, metal box toward me on the floor. There was a piece of window screen over the open top, held in place with clamps. I went over and looked. Inside were half a dozen, small lizards, sitting on sticks and crawling through a bed of wood shavings.

"These are chameleons," he said. "I got them at the parade in Lombard last Memorial Day. The man said they'd change color to match whatever they're sitting on, but it's really just different greens." He unscrewed the clamps and inched the screen back a little bit. I sat down to get a closer look. "You have to be careful when you take them out. If they get away you'll never find 'em again. They're too fast." He slid his hand into the cage, cupped it around a sleeping lizard and picked it up.

"Think fast!" he shouted, and tossed the animal at my face.

We were both surprised when I caught it. Based on past experience, I had expected something like that. Bobby was obviously disappointed. I hadn't jumped or screamed or anything. I just sat there, holding the little creature in my lap. I grinned at him, proud of my cool. He glared back.

"Nice catch," he said, "but check this out." He took another chameleon from the box and held it up, his fingers gripping it under the front legs. "Their tails grow back," he said. He glanced at the open bedroom door to make certain we were alone. Then he grabbed the lizard's tail with his other hand and jerked it off. The chameleon's mouth snapped open in a soundless scream. Its tongue bulged out of its mouth, and it closed its eyes. Bobby tossed the writhing lizard back in the cage and handed me the tail. It twitched on my palm.

"Doesn't that hurt them?" I asked. "It looks like it hurt."

"I dunno," he said. "You can keep the tail. I've got others.

I put the tail in my pocket.

Lunch consisted of baloney sandwiches and potato chips, followed by the chocolate chip cookies Mrs. Teague and Meg had baked. As she was walking around the table, refilling our empty milk glasses, Mrs. Teague paused behind Bobby's chair and rested her hand on his head. Bobby closed his eyes and leaned back, pushing the back of his head into her palm. The corners of his mouth turned up in a little smile, and he let his arms hang down at his sides. They stayed like that for a moment, and then Mrs. Teague ruffled his hair. "Go and play," she said.

The three of us kids went out back. Meg sat in a little chair on the porch and watched while Bobby and I set up a battlefield under a massive willow tree. I asked her if she wanted to come down and play with us, but she just waved. When Meg was in one of her quiet moods she could go a whole day without speaking.

Bobby had dozens of soldiers, but he had the wars all mixed together. His army was mostly little, green army men and a few medieval knights. My army was composed of Civil War soldiers, cowboys and a few spacemen. We each had one model tank. Bobby went back inside, and when he came out again he pulled a can of cigarette lighter fluid and a book of matches from under his shirt.

"Your mom's here," he said. "We'd better get crackin' if we're going to napalm these soldiers."

Fortunately our battlefield was mostly dirt, hardly any grass grew in the shade of the ancient willow. Bobby squirted lighter fluid on all the soldiers and connected the puddles at their feet with streams of the pink liquid. He took a couple of Black Cat firecrackers out of his pocket and stuck them under the tanks, then shot a thin stream of lighter fluid around their fuses. "Y'can't soak 'em," he said, "or they won't light."

He pulled a match out of the book and scraped it across the striker, cupping his hand to shield the flame from the wind. When he touched it to the lighter fluid there was a gentle whoosh, and blue flame spread from soldier to soldier, weaving across the ground until all were enveloped and, lastly, the firecracker fuses lit. The tanks blew apart, spectacularly, hurling plastic shrapnel across the yard. I got hit in the neck with a piece of a turret. The soldiers didn't burn long, and when the flames had gone out we surveyed the damage—legs sagged, facial features were smoothed to shiny nothingness, rifles and hands had melted to dripping blobs.

We got the devastated armies back in their shoebox just as my mother and Mrs. Teague stepped out onto the porch. They were holding half-empty bottles of beer, but I could tell my mother was ready to leave. She kept passing her drink from hand to hand, looking for a place to put it down. Finally, she set it on a table that held some potted plants and called to us.

"Meg, Bryan, let's go." She put her hands behind her back and turned to face Mrs. Teague. "Thank you so much for letting the kids come over. I managed to get all my little chores accomplished."

"Happy to help," Mrs. Teague said. "And Margaret and I had a nice time baking cookies. Didn't we, Margaret?"

Meg smiled up at Mrs. Teague, and my mother's mouth fell open. She must have thought Meg had been hypnotized. I clambered up the steps to the porch and fell in behind my mother, and as I did, I noticed her hands. They were covered with brown dots, some smudged and some, perfect little circles.

o

The next time we saw the Teagues was on a visit to their vacation home on Lake Geneva. Mr. Teague picked us up in the big, Greyhound bus he had bought and turned into a motor home. There was another family on the bus, a man who had been in the army with my father and Mr. Teague and his wife and daughter, who sat at the dining table in the middle of the bus with Mrs. Teague. The man sat up front with my parents so they could talk with Mr. Teague while he drove. The man was in a wheelchair and, even though he had the brakes on, he kept a grip on one of the fixed seats to keep the chair from moving around. My father rested one of his hands on the arm of the wheelchair, just in case. All the adults were wearing shorts, and you could see that the man in the wheelchair was missing his right leg from the knee down. I had never seen an amputated limb before. The skin looked taut and shiny, more like plastic than flesh. I must have been staring because, suddenly, my mother smacked me on the back of the head. "Be polite," she said.

"That's okay," the man said. "I lost my leg in Africa when I was over there with your dad. We looked all over for it, too, but we just couldn't find it." He laughed a little, with a high-pitched, nervous sort of laugh.

I stumbled to the back of the bus and sat down next to Meg on a bench that could be turned into a bed.

"I thought you'd be sitting with Mrs. Teague," I said. We both looked over at the dining table. The wheelchair man's wife and daughter were giggling at something Mrs. Teague had said.

"She's got her fan club," Meg said, and turned to look out the window.

I spent the rest of the trip trying not to stare at Mrs. Teague, then trying to not get caught staring at her. I memorized the bounce of her hair and the way she tilted her head when she was saying something serious and the bend of her thin wrist when she was gesturing with her cigarette and, especially, her open-mouthed laugh when she found something funny. I was so entranced that we were halfway to Lake Geneva before I realized Bobby wasn't on the bus.

We spent the afternoon on the private beach behind the Teagues' A-frame vacation home. My father helped wheelchair man hop across the sand to one of the beach chairs where the adults were sitting, sipping whiskey sours and talking. I curled up on a lounge near my mother, who was putting on sun tan lotion. Her face was already turning red, but it wasn't half as red as her hands. She had scrubbed them raw, trying to get the carpet dye off.

Like most of my mother's projects, she had dyed the carpet without consulting my father first. She liked to surprise him. He was surprised all right. He came home from work to find the light gray living room carpet covered with black polka dots. My mother had filled a shaker bottle with dye and walked back and forth, across the room, camouflaging her cigarette burns. When he came home that evening my father just stood in the doorway, staring at the carpet. He didn't say anything for several minutes. Meg and I watched from the kitchen and waited for the fireworks. Finally, my father looked at my mother, smiled, and said, "Hi honey. What's new?"

Mr. Teague went inside for a minute and came out with a scuba mask and snorkel. He tossed them to me.

"Here you go, Bryan, old man. These are Bobby's, but he won't mind if you use them. See what you can see at the bottom of the sea."

"Thanks, Mr. Teague," I said. "Where is Bobby? I thought he'd be here today."

Mr. Teague didn't say a word. His lips got tight, and he turned and walked back to the house. Mrs. Teague waggled her fingers at me, and I went to sit in the sand at her feet.

"Don't mind him," she said. "He's just worried about Bobby." She took a sip of her cocktail and looked out across the lake. "Bobby's trying out another military academy this weekend." She chuckled. "Or should I say they're trying him out. Anyway, Bobby may not be going to your school next year." She reached out and tousled my hair. "I'm sorry there's no one your age to play with today, but I'm sure a boy with your imagination can find something fun to do."

I sat there for a minute, aware of my skin. A tremor had started on my scalp, where her fingers touched it, and flowed down my spine and out along my limbs. Then, she shooed me away with a gesture. "Go play, now," she said. "Scoot."

Meg and the other little girl built sand castles. Meg's

was on one side of the beach, and the girl's was on the other. Occasionally the girl would walk over, look at Meg for a minute, then go back to the other side of the beach. Meg never said a word to her. The only time she acknowledged her presence was when a big speedboat tore past. It was closer to shore than it should have been, and it's wake roiled up onto the beach. Meg looked up from her work and pointed to the girl's sand castle, which was crumbling in the surf. The girl squealed and ran back to survey the damage.

I hid underwater, floating face down at the edge of a tangle of weeds and cattails, breathing through the snorkel. There were some frogs and a few sunfish hanging out in the little submerged forest. I did my best to catch one, but they were too fast for me. By the time my mother called me for dinner my back and the backs of my legs were aching and scarlet.

o

Two weeks after the trip to Lake Geneva the Teagues threw Bobby a birthday party. Most parents would have made a pizza and a birthday cake and invited a few friends over. Bobby's parents rented Kiddieland.

Kiddieland was an amusement park filled with games and rides and vendors selling hotdogs and popcorn and cotton candy. It gave kids an opportunity to eat too much, ride some spinning, zipping, whirling machine, vomit, and start the cycle again. Even with the potential for that kind of fun, Bobby was only able to get about a dozen kids to show up. Most of them were like me, kids whose parents were friends with Bobby's parents. Mr. Teague paid the owners to close the park for the day so we could have the place to ourselves.

Some of the kids brought their parents with them. My mother dropped me off with instructions to be out in the parking lot at 3 p.m. sharp, when she would return to pick me up. My father had to work, and my mother had had enough of the Teagues' "profligate exhibitionism." My parents had discussed this over dinner the night before.

"I will not subject myself to another afternoon of watching people fawn over those two. And I don't know why you insist Bryan go. He doesn't even like Bobby. He just tolerates him for your sake."

"What ever happened to showing people a little kindness?" my father asked. "They're having a difficult time. Rob was really upset when Bobby was expelled from this latest military academy."

"He tried to burn the place down, for heaven sakes. What do they expect?"

"Bobby tried to burn down a school?" I asked.

My father turned and looked at me like he just realized I was in the room. "You can't repeat any of this to anyone. Is that clear?"

"Yes," I said. "How did he do it? Burn down the school, I mean."

"He didn't burn it down. He piled up a couple of mattresses in his dormitory and set them on fire. Someone smelled the smoke, and the fire was put out before it did much damage."

"And the Dean or the General or whoever kicked Bobby out," my mother said. "His father tried to buy them off by donating a new gymnasium, but they figured if Bobby was going to end up burning it down there wasn't much point."

"The point for us," my father said, "is that they are all very upset and could use our support." He kept looking at me. I think he was afraid that if he looked at my mother he'd start yelling.

"I'll go," I said. "I don't mind."

"Really?" my mother asked.

"Really," I said. "It might be fun."

The whole group was waiting for me just inside the entrance. I was the last one to arrive. Mrs. Teague was all in white—blouse, skirt, and tennis shoes. She smiled at me, but when she turned around Bobby punched me in the arm. "You're late, man," he said. "I didn't think you were coming."

We were really too old for most of the rides; they were designed for kids about Meg's age, but we made the most of it. There were games with prizes like Ring Toss and Pitch Out, and there was plenty of food. The best part was that Bobby's father had paid for it all in advance. There were no lines either. If you wanted to go on a ride you just walked up and rode it. Bobby spent most of his time throwing darts at balloons. The man who ran the game must have been paid off because no matter how many balloons Bobby popped, he always won a big stuffed animal. I divided most of my time between the Tilt-A-Whirl and the roller coaster. These were the only two rides for older kids in the park, and they were good ones. The Tilt-A-Whirl could easily make you lose your lunch and the roller coaster had a sharp turn followed by a sixty-foot drop. It was called the Big Dipper, and I had been afraid to ride it up until I was ten years old.

I took a break for lunch and got a hotdog and a root

beer. I saw Mrs. Teague sitting alone on a bench, watching Bobby play the Ring Toss game. I sat next to her, but she was watching so intently she didn't notice me at first. I followed her gaze to see Bobby hurling rings at the pegs. He never got a ringer. The wooden rings hit the table with a whack and bounced up in the air or caromed off and landed in the midway. The man running the game just stood and watched. He looked confused. Bobby hurled ring after ring, as hard as he could. I turned to say something to Mrs. Teague, but she was crying. She didn't make any noise, but her cheeks were wet, and she clenched her purse while she rocked back and forth on the bench.

When Bobby ran out of rings he looked around and saw us watching him. He left his pile of stuffed animals in front of the Ring Toss and came to sit with us. He was breathing hard, and his cheeks were flushed.

"Scoot on over," he said, sliding in between his mother and me. "Man, did you see that? I swear, that game is fixed."

Mrs. Teague took a handkerchief out of her purse and blotted her eyes. "Well dear," she started, "perhaps an underhand toss might have been more…"

Her mild scolding was drowned out by the arrival of the rest of the group. Mr. Teague and the other parents and kids were having a popcorn battle. They were laughing and tossing handfuls of popcorn at one another. When they saw us sitting on the bench they attacked, hurling fistfuls of the fluffy stuff in the air over our heads. It was a salty, imitation-buttery, blizzard. I started eating popcorn off my lap, which cracked everyone up.

"Hey," Mr. Teague shouted, "who's up for one last ride

on the Big Dipper?"

I looked at my watch. It was almost three o'clock, but I couldn't pass up one more ride. Only a few of us wanted to go. We hurried over to the loading ramp and paired up. Mr. Teague sat in the front car with one of the girls. She was frightened and wanted to ride with an adult. I looked for Mrs. Teague, but she was leading Bobby toward the last car in the line. I wound up sitting with a kid I had never met before. The attendant went from car to car, lowering the lap bar and telling us to stay seated. The lap bar was hinged on one end and, after he pulled it across our laps, the attendant secured the other end with a big metal pin. When he was finished he stepped back, released the brake, and we were off, clattering up the track, past the crisscross of wooden beams and braces.

The coaster ran through a series of small dips and turns before it began the main ascent. On the straight-aways we thrust our hands into the air. We screamed and yelled as the ground changed places with the sky. On the curves we snatched our hands back, anxiously gripping the lap bar when it felt like inertia would hurl us off into the void. But we were quiet as we approached the top of the highest run. I looked up at the blue and felt the wind ruffle my hair. There was a shriek from someone behind me and then the drop. We dove toward the earth, and the kid next to me was clutching my arm, and I couldn't tell if I was laughing or screaming. And then it was over. The cars glided up to the platform and stopped, but someone was still screaming. Bobby had fallen out at the top of the coaster.

Mr. Teague rode with Bobby in the ambulance to the

hospital. Mrs. Teague stayed behind to wait with the children whose parents hadn't come to pick them up yet. I went out to the parking lot and asked my mother for another ten minutes, then went back to wait with Mrs. Teague. She was sitting on the same midway bench where we had watched Bobby at the Ring Toss booth. Dressed in white, encircled by the white popcorn that still covered the ground, she looked like a very sad angel. One of the girls was lying on the bench with her head on Mrs. Teague's lap. I sat on the grass, behind the bench, and waited. After a few minutes the girl's father arrived and waved to her from the entrance. She ran to him, and they walked out together, toward the parking lot.

Mrs. Teague looked at me and stood up. "Is your mother here, yet, Bryan?" she asked.

I nodded.

"All right, then," she said. "Tell her I said hello." She turned and walked away, toward the bathrooms. I watched her go. Her shoulders were slumped and her arms hung down at her sides. As she walked, she reached into the pocket of her skirt, pulled something out, and dropped it in the grass. I waited until the washroom door closed behind her, and then went to see what she had dropped. It was a big metal pin. The kind used to secure a lap bar on the Big Dipper.

○

I never saw Bobby Teague, or any of the Teagues, again. Bobby died on the operating table. My father said the brain damage had been so severe that it was just as well. It was a little over a month after the funeral that Mrs. Teague went to live with her mother, somewhere on the east coast. She filed for divorce shortly after that. My father still got together with

Mr. Teague, usually for drinks and dinner with wheelchair man, but that eventually ended, too. Mr. Teague sold the Cadillac dealership and moved out to Los Angeles.

    I kept the metal pin. It's in a box, along with a desiccated chameleon tail and a few other childhood mementos, on a shelf down in the basement.

Tim Chapman is a former forensic scientist for the Chicago police department who currently teaches writing and tai chi chuan. He holds a Master's degree in Creative Writing from Northwestern University. His short fiction has been published in The Southeast Review, the Chicago Reader, Alfred Hitchcock's Mystery Magazine, Chicago Tribune's Printers Row Journal, and the anthology, *The Rich and the Dead*. His first novel, *Bright and Yellow, Hard and Cold*, was a finalist in Shelf Unbound's 2013 Best Indie Book competition. In his spare time he paints pretty pictures and makes an annoying noise with his saxophone that he claims is music. He lives in Chicago with his lovely and patient wife, Ellen, and Mia, the squirrel-chasingest dog in town.

Praise for *Bright and Yellow, Hard and Cold*

"A story this complex is hard to pull off, but author Chapman has the right stuff. A former forensic scientist himself, he knows that in a good novel crimes aren't committed by cardboard characters, and they aren't solved by them, either. The best fiction reveals great truths, and there are plenty to be had in Bright and Yellow, Hard and Cold. My favorite comes from McKinney: 'Law is man's attempt to civilize society. Science is man's attempt to reveal truth. Forensic science, then, is the intersection of civilization and truth.'" —Betty Webb, Mystery Scene

"Chapman brings scientific realism and very human passions to work in his first novel, a thoroughly engaging thriller." —Steve Steinbock, Ellery Queen's Mystery Magazine

"…combines the author's trademark forensic authenticity with a vivid historical mystery to offer compelling portraits of Chicago crime in two eras." —Linda Landrigan, Editor of Alfred Hitchcock's Mystery Magazine

"McKinney is a complicated hero, absolutely at home fighting the system. An intriguing and enlightening read." —Connie Fletcher, Booklist

"Bright and Yellow, Hard and Cold has a unique crime story to tell, keeps it gripping, and makes one wonder what Mr. Chapman has up his sleeve for the next novel." —James Burt, ForeWord Reviews

"In its simplest, this is Chapman's ode to the forensic scientist, but if you dig deep there are facets of Bright and Yellow, Hard and Cold that will have you questioning what effect greed has on us all." —Alan Senatore, Cold Hill Review

CPSIA information can be obtained at www.ICGtesting.com
Printed in the USA
LVOW11s1325031016
507195LV00003B/186/P